Cast of Characters

Henry Debbon. A young attorney, he's [...] at the Boster law firm. He's been assign[...] red-headed stepdaughter from an esca[...]

Diana Herron. The stepdaughter. She seems a bit confused by Henry's attentions, but as long as he's willing to pay for the taxis she isn't about to complain.

Claude Boster. Diana's stepfather and boss to Henry. He adores Diana but doesn't think much of Henry and thinks even less of encouraging any romance between the two young people.

Fred Boster. Claude's slacker son, he's been packed off to France.

Ted. A struggling young doctor who has the misfortune to be Henry's friend. He thinks Diana is quite a dish and if Henry doesn't make a move, he will.

Evans. Boster's right-hand man, he's never late for work and never complains. He also disappears. Nobody remembers his first name.

Mrs. Evans. His wife, she's a good cook (Boster disagrees) who sees spirits, including Henry's dead aunt.

Miss Robb. "Robby" to Henry, she's Boster's beautiful, coolly efficient private secretary. She likes a good time and has a little fun at Henry's expense.

Scrimmer. An escaped convict who Boster says is out to get him—and his family—because he refused to represent him.

Gilling. He'a a tough cop who appears without warning at just about every juncture.

Mae. That's Mae, spelled M-A-E. She's a tough nurse who hides Henry's clothes.

Auntie. Henry's aunt. She's dead but that doesn't stop her from enjoying a glass of sherry from time to time.

Books by Constance & Gwenyth Little

The Grey Mist Murders (1938)*
Black-Headed Pins (1938)*
The Black Gloves (1939)*
Black Corridors (1940)*
The Black Paw (1941)*
The Black Shrouds (1941)*
The Black Thumb (1942)*
The Black Rustle (1943)*
The Black Honeymoon (1944)*
Great Black Kanba (1944)*
The Black Eye (1945)*
The Black Stocking (1946)*
The Black Goatee (1947)*
The Black Coat (1948)*
The Black Piano (1948)*
The Black House (1950)*
The Black Smith (1950)
The Blackout (1951)
The Black Dream (1952)
The Black Iris (1953)
The Black Curl (1953)

*reprinted by the Rue Morgue Press
as of June 2004

The Black House

by Constance & Gwenyth Little

Rue Morgue Press
Boulder / Lyons

Printed at Johnson Printing
Boulder, Colorado

The Rue Morgue Press
P.O. Box 4119
Boulder, CO 80306

PRINTED IN THE UNITED STATES OF AMERICA

About the Littles

Although all but one of their books had "black" in the title, the 21 mysteries of Constance (1899-1980) and Gwenyth (1903-1985) Little were far from somber affairs. The two Australian-born sisters from East Orange, New Jersey, were far more interested in coaxing chuckles than in inducing chills from their readers.

Indeed, after their first book, *The Grey Mist Murders*, appeared in 1938, Constance rebuked an interviewer for suggesting that their murders weren't realistic by saying, "Our murderers strangle. We have no sliced-up corpses in our books." However, as the books mounted, the Littles did go in for all sorts of gruesome murder methods—"horrible," was the way their own mother described them—which included the occasional sliced-up corpse.

But the murders were always off stage and tempered by comic scenes in which bodies and other objects, including swimming pools, were constantly disappearing and reappearing. The action took place in large old mansions, boarding houses, hospitals, hotels, or on trains or ocean liners, anywhere the Littles could gather together a large cast of eccentric characters, many of whom seemed to have escaped from a Kaufman play or a Capra movie. The typical Little heroine—each book was a stand-alone—often fell under suspicion herself and turned detective to keep the police from slapping the cuffs on. Whether she was a working woman or a spoiled little rich brat, she always spoke her mind, kept her rather sarcastic sense of humor, and got her man, both murderer and husband. But if marriage was in the offing, it was always on her terms and the vows were taken with more than a touch of cynicism. Love was grand, but it was even grander if the husband could either pitch in with the cooking and cleaning or was wealthy enough to hire household help.

The Littles wrote all their books in bed—"Chairs give one backaches," Gwenyth complained—with Constance providing detailed plot outlines while Gwenyth did the final drafts. Over the years that pattern changed somewhat, but Constance always insisted that Gwen "not mess up my clues." Those clues were everywhere, and the Littles made sure there were no loose ends. Seemingly irrelevant events were revealed to be of major significance in the final summation. The plots were often preposterous, a fact often recognized by both the Littles and their characters, all of whom seem to be winking at the reader, almost as if sharing a private joke. You just have to accept the fact that there are different natural laws in the wacky universe created by these sisters. There are no other mystery writers quite like them. At times, their books seem to be an odd collaboration between P.G. Wodehouse and Cornell Woolrich.

The present volume, *The Black House*, is the first to be told primarily from a male point of view, perhaps because the post-World War II book market was increasingly aimed at a male audience or perhaps simply because the Littles themselves wanted a change. However, readers will recognize in Henry Debbon all of the features of the typical Little heroine, including a heavy reliance on sarcasm. Henry is also probably a bit more belligerent than any of their female leads and actually shows an inclination to be somewhat of an action hero, although the results resemble the silent movie Keystone Cops more than the hard-boiled novels of Dashiell Hammett. Diana, the beautiful, redheaded female lead, threatens, from time to time, to match him barb for barb, but she mostly accepts her supporting role. Other Little books from this postwar period also showed departures from the tried-and-true formulas of the 1930s and earlier 1940s. *The Black Piano*, for example, is far darker than any other Little novel. Although it presents one of their most inventive plots, there is little of that sparkling byplay between the heroine and her would-be suitor that was so evident in the earlier books. They also experiment with style, including a relatively successful experiment with multiple point of view in *The Black Goatee*.

The Littles published their two final novels, *The Black Curl* and *The Black Iris*, in 1953, and if they missed writing after that, they were at least able to devote more time to their real passion—traveling. The two made at least three trips around the world at a time when that would have been a major undertaking. For more information on the Littles and their books, see the introductions by Tom & Enid Schantz to The Rue Morgue Press editions of *The Black Gloves* and *The Black Honeymoon*.

Chapter 1

HENRY DEBBON gave himself a last hasty glance in the mirror and hurried out of his hotel room, his arms shrugging frantically into his flying overcoat. In the elevator, he had a more leisurely look into the narrow mirror at the back and was relieved to see that his tie was on and that there were no spots of shaving soap lingering about his ears. It was these lousy late nights, he thought gloomily—and women, on pleasure bent, who did not have to get up in the morning.

He went out into the street and immediately hailed a cab, but it didn't stop. He looked after it, snarling softly, and then dashed for the subway. He couldn't afford to take a cab every morning, anyway.

He was unable to get any sleep in the subway because it was too crowded, and he crawled into the building that housed the office of his boss, Claude Boster, with a pallid feeling that the day before him was all too long. A quick glance at his watch assured him that he was just making it, and he stepped into the elevator with a long breath of achievement. The operator, a stripling with a sophisticated eye, put his gum to rest for a moment and observed, "Early this morning, ain'tcha, Mr. Debbon?"

Henry, scenting sarcasm, nevertheless responded with a courteous murmur because he feared the youth's tongue. He stepped out into the corridor, wondering irritably why Claude must needs get into the office before his employees, sometimes as much as an hour before them. There must be something wrong with a boss who would do that, instead

7

of wandering in elegantly an hour later and thus giving his employees a little leeway. But Claude was always there, chewing on his cigar and taking note of each slave who came in. No one, Henry thought, as he approached the door, would get him in before ten when he was running an office, if he ever would.

The door was locked. It took him a moment or two to realize this, and then he stood and looked at the frosted glass panel before him almost stupidly. Claude had not arrived, but then no one else had either, and that was impossible. Perhaps they were playing a joke on him. He pulled his key ring out of his pocket and slowly sorted out the office key. It had been given to him in the event of occasional night work, but so far he'd been able to duck that. Not that there was much to duck. The old man was giving him only the dumb stuff to handle. And that was going to bear bitter fruit for the old man someday, because no firm should be a one-man proposition, and Henry Debbon was quite capable of handling the most intricate problems. All he needed was a chance.

The office was completely deserted, and Henry stopped, with his hand still on the door, and sent a wild glance at the clock. He stared at it for a moment, and then looked at his own watch and groaned loudly. So that was it. He'd wrenched himself from his bed, done a hasty and improper dressing job, and come down here without breakfast, all because he couldn't read a lousy watch properly. One whole lousy hour too early.

Well, he could go and get breakfast. But he decided against that almost immediately. For once, when Mr. Claude Boster arrived, he would see his brilliant assistant there before him, working earnestly. He could get breakfast when he usually had it, which was directly after Claude went out for his morning coffee. In fact, they all turned out for coffee at that time, with the single exception of old Evans, who was still the conscientious type after thirty years of being confronted by the fact that it got him nowhere.

Henry sighed and began to busy himself with the usual dumb stuff. At the sound of approaching footsteps he dropped his head lower and assumed a deep interest in what lay before him, but when the door opened, he knew at once that it was not Claude who had come in. He looked up and saw a thin man with sparse hair and a pockmarked face.

Henry stood up, trying to look every inch a lawyer, but the man brushed past him, muttering something about an appointment, and made for Claude's office.

"Mr. Boster is not in yet," Henry said, taking a step or two after him. "Will you wait out here, please?"

The stranger, evidently a man of few words, replied tersely, "No, I won't," and went into Claude's office, shutting the door firmly behind him.

Henry shrugged and returned to the dumb stuff and was still immersed in it when Claude walked in a short time later. Claude stopped dead just inside the door and observed in his usual booming voice, "Good God! What happened! Did you get locked in last night?"

Henry said coldly, "Good morning, Mr. Boster," and continued to move his pen across the paper.

Claude, chewing on his customary cigar, looked him over. "I suppose you were so bleary-eyed this morning that you read your watch wrong." This was so astutely the truth that Henry was more bitterly offended than if he had merely come down early to get some work done.

He said, with remote and frigid courtesy, "There is a man waiting for you in your office."

Claude glanced at the closed door of his office. "Nonsense, it's too early. You're not awake yet. Have you had coffee?"

"I—er—"

Claude nodded. "That's what I thought. Go on down and get some. And have it black and strong. I have something important for you today." He swung across to his office and went in, shutting the door with a slight crash.

Henry sent an evil look after him, but only when the door had closed. Claude was big and fat, he reflected, but he could move quickly enough when he wanted to. Oh, well, better get some breakfast. He looked down at the work in front of him and decided to finish this particular piece first. He might as well get it out of the way, and then he could enjoy his coffee.

Old Evans, the bookkeeper, was the next to arrive, and Henry glanced up at him without interest. Always early, never absent, often worked late, and to this very day Claude never could remember so much as his first name.

They exchanged greetings, and Evans added, "You're early this morning, Mr. Debbon."

Henry's pen was already in motion again, and he muttered sourly, "I'm turning over a new leaf."

Claude opened his door and, after an uninterested glance and a brief nod at Evans, turned on Henry and barked, "I thought you said there was a man waiting for me in here."

"Certainly I did," Henry replied stiffly. "He said he had an appointment and went in and shut the door."

"You must have had a night out, boy," Claude observed tolerantly. "You'd better go and get your coffee. There's no one here."

"Then you'd better look down and see if there's a crowd on the sidewalk," Henry muttered. "He must have jumped out the window."

But Claude had already slammed back into his office, and almost immediately the two girls came in together. Miss Robb, tall, dark and always exquisitely neat and clean, was Claude's private secretary. She was pretty, but not so lively as Cissy, who was a clerk and more or less girl of all work. Cissy had flyaway blond curls and a freckled nose. They were exactly on time, and Cissy began talking at once, which was usual. She rarely stopped and was undaunted by the fact that no one ever listened. Miss Robb, walking lightly and glistening with cleanliness, disappeared into Claude's office.

It was Monday, and Cissy began to give a detailed account of her weekend. It was a long story and was necessarily interrupted now and then, but she had got as far as Sunday evening when Claude pounded through on his way to his morning coffee. Cissy fell silent until he had closed the outer door behind him, and then she heaved a long sigh. "He's early today, and am I ever thankful! After a weekend like I had, I'm dying!"

Henry saw that it was not quite ten o'clock and thankfully pushed his work to one side. He was glad he hadn't gone out earlier. He could really enjoy some breakfast now. Miss Robb glided in, and Evans gave them the usual sourly reproachful look as they trooped out, but no one noticed him. As the door closed behind them, he bent closer over his books, with his mouth in a thin line.

Downstairs in the coffee shop Henry and the two girls were joined by Fred Boster, who was Claude's son. He never came to work much before eleven and usually left at about four, but no one objected, since he did nothing in the office but get in everyone's way. However, Claude preferred to think that he was a smart boy and told the others so at stated intervals, but this was generally regarded as bravado and, as such, was more or less ignored.

Fred slipped into a chair at their table now and said sunnily, "I'm going to tell the old man on you all someday—the entire office force lounging around at ten in the morning, lapping up coffee."

"Oh, shut up," Miss Robb said languidly. "He's lucky to have us, and he knows it. We can get jobs anywhere."

Cissy giggled, and Fred squinted at Miss Robb across a fork he was balancing on the end of his finger. "Honey chile, why are you always so cold to me?"

Honey chile Robb called for another coffee. "We'd all go any time we wanted to, only for our kind hearts. He remembers the days when the boss was the big noise, and we let him think it's still so."

Cissy and Fred both began to talk at once, and since neither would give ground, they went on in chorus until Miss Robb looked at her watch and stood up immediately. She swept the others with a glance and said, "Come on, he left early, so he'll probably be back early."

Fred tried to pull her down again with a hand on her arm. "Don't go yet. You fellas can all get other jobs, so to hell with him."

"Certainly we can get other jobs," Henry agreed, "but you can't, and you're supposed to show up right after morning coffee."

Miss Robb was already moving off, and Fred followed reluctantly. "O.K., I suppose you're right, and anyway old Evans might have to go to the you-know-what and he'd never leave the office alone."

Cissy began to giggle hysterically until Miss Robb put a stop to it by saying simply, "Dick."

Cissy sobered at once, smoothed her flyaway curls, and moved sedately, but when they were in the elevator, she whispered tensely, "Where was he? I didn't see him."

"He saw you," Miss Robb assured her composedly.

The telephone was ringing angrily when they got back to the office, and as Cissy snatched it up, Henry looked around with a bewildered expression. The outer office was empty, so was Claude's room, and, in fact, Evans seemed to have disappeared.

Chapter 2

HENRY, HIS forehead wrinkled in a puzzled frown, jabbed Fred in the ribs and said, "Old Evans seems to have disappeared."

Fred, who was looking at Miss Robb, murmured absently, "Evans? He's probably off getting a shampoo and wave."

Henry went back to his work. He felt sure that Evans would never leave the office empty unless, after all these years, it had suddenly occurred to him that he was a worm and had better turn. Only he wouldn't simply get up and walk out. He'd go to Claude, announce his grievance, and then depart. Anyway, it didn't matter. No doubt the old mossback would show up eventually with an explanation.

Henry yawned, shifted his weight on his chair, and wondered what Claude had up his sleeve. What he was going to give him today that was important to do? He was just plugging along here, and not getting anywhere, sort of a glorified clerk, that was all. After all, he was a lawyer and an experienced lawyer at that. Why had he accepted Claude's offer, anyway? The other had been a much bigger concern, and he might have got somewhere there. But this had looked better to him, working up to be a partner someday, and then taking over when Claude retired. He hadn't known about Fred, of course, and the way it looked now, Fred would be shoved in at the top, with Henry sitting at his right hand doing all the brainwork.

The office droned on through a slow morning, and neither Claude nor Evans returned. Henry waited while the others went to lunch, and just before two o'clock, when he was thinking of having his own, Claude walked in. Henry approached him and said rather formally, "Mr. Boster, Mr. Evans seems to have disappeared."

Claude shifted his cigar from one side of his mouth to the other. "Disappeared? Who's disappeared?"

"Mr. Evans. He hasn't been in the office for some hours, and I was wondering if you'd sent him on an errand."

"Talk sense," said Claude impatiently. "I never send Evans on errands. Go and look in the can. Maybe he's sick." He brushed past

Henry and called to Fred, "Come into my office, boy. I've something to tell you."

Henry went along to the men's room, found it empty, and returned to the office. Cissy looked up at him and asked wonderingly, "Isn't he there? But where in the world could he be? I mean, he's always here."

Miss Robb and Fred emerged from Claude's office, and Miss Robb gave Henry a significant look. "Mr. Boster wishes to see you, and he's simply seething about something."

"No, he isn't," Fred contradicted her amiably. "That's just Force and Drive. He's always like that when he has an iron or two in the fire."

Henry went in and closed the door behind him, and Claude waved him to a seat. "Now, I told you this morning that I had something important for you. I don't say you're going to like it—it's tough, and I'll admit it—but if you handle it successfully, I'll load you up with plenty of the stuff that you really like doing. In fact, you'll be practically a partner. I've watched your work, and it's good. I'm going to need you. Fred's no good as a lawyer—might as well face it—so he's going to do the things he likes from now on. I'm going to give him every chance to follow his own pursuits—" Claude paused and stared at the window for a moment without appearing to see it, after which he cleared his throat thunderously and turned back to frown at Henry. "You're going places around here, son, but you'll have to do this job for me first."

Henry sat up straighter and tried not to look like a boy being presented with a new bike. He said, "Thank you very much, sir. I shall be glad to handle this job for you."

Claude munched on his cigar for a while and then observed with apparent irrelevance, "Fred's hopping a boat for France."

Henry looked a bit puzzled, and Claude added, "This afternoon."

"This afternoon?"

"Going to dabble in something or other in Paris."

"Oh, Paris."

"He was going anyway in a week or two, so I told him he might as well get off this afternoon. Matter of fact, Pitty Scrimmer has escaped."

"Who?"

"Never mind, Claude said irritably. "This man has escaped from prison, and he swore to do me damage of some kind because I refused to take his case when he was put in."

"But—"

"I know, I know, I'm not a criminal lawyer, but the guy latched onto me and I couldn't make him understand that we don't handle cases of that sort."

"I see."

"So now he's escaped, and Fred's taking off for Paris this afternoon."

"That's fine," Henry said heartily. "Fred ought to be safe. But what about you?"

"Ahh!" Claude leaned back in his chair and stretched his fat legs out in front of him. He made a very rude comment on the sinister Mr. Scrimmer, and added, "I'm not afraid of him. I know what he looks like. But there's Diana."

"Diana ?"

"For God's sake!" Claude yelled. "Stop repeating everything I say. Yes, Diana!"

In an effort not to repeat everything Claude said, Henry remained silent.

Claude, a hard man to please at times, was further annoyed. "Well, don't just sit there like a stuffed rabbit!"

Henry stirred and cleared his throat. "Yes, of course—Diana. Why don't you simply put her on the boat with Fred? Or is she—er—a new wife?"

Claude's face went a dull purple, and he shouted, "Godammit, I'm going to have more respect around here! Who d'ya think you're talking to? You act as though I had a new wife every year. She is *not* a new wife! She's my daughter."

"Oh no, she isn't," Henry retorted, stung into doing battle in spite of the rosy future that had been dangled before him. "I happen to know that you don't have a daughter."

Claude grunted, and the purple faded out of his face. "She's the daughter of my second wife, and I look upon her as my own. She lives with her mother, but she often visits me, and she's always called me Papa. She's fond of me too. What more d'ya want?"

"She's your daughter," Henry said dutifully.

Claude heaved a vast sigh. "She's staying with me now, and I'm worried about her. I tell you I couldn't stand it if anything happened to her."

Henry wished that he could go out and get his lunch, but he didn't like to say so.

Claude fished a fresh cigar froth his pocket and turned it over in his fingers. "You'll have to watch over her and see that she doesn't come to any harm."

Henry closed his mouth, which had fallen open, and subsequently tried to keep the fury out of his face and voice. He said carefully, "You want me to trot around after a girl on my flat feet with a gun in my hip pocket and a toothpick in my vest pocket? Pity you couldn't have told me earlier so that I needn't have wasted four years and a lot of money going through college."

Claude, chewing violently on the fresh cigar, made an obvious effort to get his temper under control.

"I'm asking this as a special favor to me, Henry," he said presently. "I couldn't trust anyone else I'd be able to get, and I love that girl. She means a hell of a lot to me. It won't be for long. Just until they catch this guy. The police always pick them up quickly."

"Because that's their job," Henry said bitterly, "and they undoubtedly know more about bodyguarding than I do too."

"Nothing of the sort. Now listen, I want somebody to be with her all the time, but I don't want her to know anything about it, because she might be frightened. I'll introduce you to her, and you can pretend to fall hard, so that you'll have an excuse for hanging around."

"Oh, certainly," Henry said coldly. "And what will my girlfriend say if she finds out? A fellow could ruin his whole life that way."

"Damn your silly girlfriend!" Claude yelled, losing the temper which he had struggled for so long to control.

Henry looked down at the toes of his shoes and made a vast attempt to look sorrowful, but a smile had begun to flirt with the corners of his mouth.

Claude shifted his considerable weight in the swivel chair and had another try at being courteous. "I'm sorry, of course, but when you see Diana, I'm sure you won't find it such a difficult assignment. She has the most beautiful red hair that you or anyone has ever seen."

"Are you trying to make a match?" Henry asked innocently.

Claude denied it with a roar that rattled the windows. "Godammit, do you think I'd let her marry you? What's the matter with you? I think you're purposely trying to irritate me, because I've asked you to do me a trifling favor. For God's sake let's get down to business here. I suppose you've had your lunch?"

"No," said Henry, glad that the point had been raised.

Claude muttered, "Good!" and reached for the phone.

Half an hour later Henry found himself seated opposite Diana Herron in a restaurant. Claude had been right about the hair—it was beautiful—but the girl herself seemed to be the quiet type. He wondered gloomily why she didn't read those columns which tell girls how to keep the conversation going by asking the man what sports interested him and so on. This gave him an idea, so he asked her what sports she was interested in.

Diana said, "None," and gazed at something over Henry's right shoulder.

"Do you care for music?" Henry asked desperately.

"No."

Food was brought to them, and they ate in silence. When Henry finally had to abandon his plate because it was empty, he fell back on the weather.

"I hear we're due for a snowstorm."

"Really?"

"Yes. Er—do you like snow?"

Diana picked up her bag and gloves and said, "I have a doctor's appointment in fifteen minutes. I'll have to go."

Henry drew a long breath of relief and dutifully guided her outside, where he hailed a cab. He handed her in and climbed in after her.

She looked at him, and after a blank moment asked, "Are you coming too?"

"Yes," Henry said glumly.

"Why?"

"I—well, as a matter of fact I have the afternoon off, and when you've finished with the doctor, we can go somewhere and have a drink."

"Oh no, we can't," the girl said firmly. "You ought to be ashamed of yourself, hanging around me this way, just to advance yourself at the office."

Henry felt his ears burning, and resorted to a cold dignity. "It's a perfectly sound business procedure. All my boy friends do the same sort of thing, and it's the only way a young man can get on in the world."

Diana was silent for a moment, and then she gave forth a pretty trill of laughter. Henry, silently loathing Claude, remained unamused.

"Did Papa give you enough money to pay for the taxi?" the girl asked presently. "I'm a bit broke myself."

Henry nodded. "I can also give you a cocktail or two, with the theater later on."

"No." She shook her red head with decision. "I have another date after I'm through with the doctor, and you might as well go home or pick up your own date, if you want to. I won't tell on you."

"Would you be good enough to shut up?" Henry asked courteously.

She tried to prevent him from going into the doctor's waiting room, but he pushed in behind her doggedly. They found two straight, uncomfortable chairs, picked up magazines, and read in silence. Henry was deep in an interesting article which stated for a fact that women were growing steadily more intelligent while men were becoming more clothheaded by the minute when Diana was called into the doctor's office. At the same time a man walked into the waiting room, and Henry peered around the edge of his magazine and eyed him narrowly. He was well dressed, with a quiet manner, but his face had the undeniable stamp of the gangster. Henry, without lowering the magazine, continued to watch him carefully. He felt that it was important for a lawyer like himself to be able to place people simply by looking at them, and it was part of the current job to keep an eye out for characters such as this one, even though Claude had probably exaggerated the whole thing.

The nurse, who had been pounding a typewriter at her desk, stood up and said, "You can come in now, Mr. Yasher."

The gangster followed her to the regions of hideously gleaming glass and chromium, and she came back alone, leaving him to his fate. She sat down at her desk and then swung around to ask Henry in a confidential tone, "You know who he is?"

Henry said, "No," and tried to look bored.

"That's Zog K. Yasher, the famous violinist."

Henry said, "That so?" and felt himself blushing. He added hastily, "Warm in here, isn't it?"

She seemed affronted and began to fuss around the room, looking at thermometers. In the end she stated coldly that the temperature was exactly as the doctor liked to have it in the waiting room.

Diana emerged from the inner sanctum accompanied by the doctor, who was saying something about a hospital. She replied, "All right, I'll be there. See you later," and walked out. Henry was sorry to abandon the article on the comparative intelligence of men and women, but the nurse was watching him, so he dropped the magazine and hastened after Diana.

"Are you going into a hospital?" he asked.

She nodded. "Memorial Hospital. This afternoon."

"What are they going to do to you?"

"I've decided to have my hair amputated. The latest trend is toward the short bob."

"How long do you expect to be there?"

She was climbing into a taxi by this time and did not bother to answer.

"Do you always take taxis like this?" he asked, crowding in after her.

"Only when you're around, oiled up as you are with Papa's money."

"Can't you tell me how long you'll be in the hospital?"

"Well, I'm really sorry about that," she said mildly. "Only a day and two nights. It won't be much of a vacation for you."

Henry sighed, and wondered how on earth he was going to watch the girl while she was in the hospital. It was impossible. They'd throw him out, naturally. Well, he'd tell Claude. The old man couldn't expect miracles. Only that was just the trouble. The old crumb expected you to do what he wanted done, whether it was impossible or not.

Diana left him to pay the taxi and tripped up the steps of Claude's small, expensive town house. She put a key into the front door, slipped inside, and shut it almost in Henry's face. He looked at the blank panels for a moment, and then descended the steps and made his way to a drugstore on the next corner. He telephoned Claude, and after explaining all the circumstances very reasonably, had to stand in silence for some time while Claude made a lot of absurd statements. He ended the harangue by shouting, "You're to be at the hospital, watching her, as long as she is there, or you're fired! Get it?"

Henry got it and longed to say, "I quit," but Claude's earlier promises held him silent. He hung up and returned to the street, picking up a toothpick from the counter on the way. He stood on the corner for a while, chewing moodily on the toothpick and reflecting that if he were going to be a lousy dick, he might as well look like one.

He realized after a while that it was growing much colder, and he turned up the collar of his coat, and then suddenly he swung back into the drugstore and returned to the phone booth.

He called up a friend of his, a young doctor just starting out in practice, and said rather abruptly, "I want to go to the hospital, Ted."

"Oh, shut up," Ted said peevishly. "I wish you wouldn't phone me up for nothing. I always think it's a patient, and the disappointment is telling on my health."

"Don't offend me," Henry warned him. "I am a patient, and I want to go to the Memorial Hospital tonight. You'd better get busy and arrange it."

"What'd the matter with you?"

"Checkup," said Henry.

"Checkup?"

"Yes, checkup. Didn't that lousy college you went to ever tell you what a checkup means?"

"Listen," Ted said reasonably, "you don't have to go to the hospital for a checkup. I can give you one here in my office—absolutely guaranteed to be the best obtainable."

"I won't come near your piffling little office, and you can tell me now whether you'll arrange this thing for me, or shall I take my money elsewhere?"

"Where's your pain?" Ted asked mildly.

"I haven't got any Goddamned pain! I want a checkup, and I want to go to the Memorial Hospital in about half an hour."

"O.K., O.K., the customer is always right. You can have your checkup, bless your little heart. I'll phone you which hospital and what day of what week I can arrange for you."

"Listen," Henry said, with sudden deadly calm, *"I'll* phone *you* in half an hour, and if you haven't arranged for me to go into the Memorial Hospital—and *only* the Memorial Hospital—tonight you have lost a patient."

"Yes, sir," Ted bleated, "yes, sir, of course. Who do you think I am? I couldn't even get myself in there tonight if I were bleeding from a thousand wounds."

"Are you going to try?" Henry asked ominously.

"Yes, dammit, I'm going to try, but I assure you—"

Henry hung up, left the drugstore, and walked moodily down toward Claude's house. A sprinkling of people were walking on both sides of the street, and although they all looked harmless, he admitted glumly to himself that after his mistake in the doctor's office his opinion on that score was not very valuable.

A cab stopped before the Boster house, and Claude emerged and hurried up the steps. Henry, whose feet were getting cold, hurried up after him and just managed to squeeze inside before the door was closed with Claude's usual vigorous bang.

Claude turned around and glowered at him. "Oh, it's you. Why aren't you watching her?"

"I am watching her."

"Then where in hell is she?"

"Upstairs in her bedroom," Henry said, since that seemed the most likely.

Claude made for the stairs and pounded up, and Henry followed, hoping for the best.

Diana was in her bedroom, packing a small suitcase, and Claude asked at once, "What's this about your going to the hospital, baby?"

"How in the world did you hear that?" Diana asked, and added, as she caught sight of Henry, "Oh, of course. Fido told you."

"But what is it? What's the matter?" Claude yelled agitatedly.

"Calm down, Papa." She closed the suitcase and smiled reassuringly at him. "It's nothing serious, merely a polyp in my nose which has to be removed. The doctor was good enough to wedge me in the hospital tonight, and I'll be out day after tomorrow.'

"But why do it in such a hurry?" Claude asked, unhappy and still agitated. "You should get another opinion first."

"Darling," she said, "do stop worrying. It's nothing at all, and I'm glad to get it over with as soon as possible. Now, let's go down and have a drink. I needn't leave for about half an hour."

"That's a good idea," Henry said approvingly and was a bit taken aback when they both turned and stared coldly at him. He stopped smiling and headed for the stairs. "All right," he said, "you needn't make it any plainer. I'll go out into the back yard with my pail and shovel."

They both called him back, Claude with a warning snarl and Diana with a hint of remorse. She said, quite kindly, "We'll all have cocktails. I'll mix them myself."

They went downstairs, and Diana and Henry entered the small, luxuriously furnished drawing room. Diana opened a cabinet and began to sort bottles, and Claude went off to the kitchen for some ice.

Henry moved over to the cabinet and stooped a little to ask the girl if he could help her. At the same time a hot, searing pain streaked the side of his face, and he lifted his hand, dazedly, to his cheek. It came away smeared with blood.

Chapter 3

THE ONLY NOISE had been a tiny pinging sound, and apparently Diana had heard nothing, for she did not raise her head from the array of bottles. Henry looked at the wall and saw a bullet hole, fresh and sinister. The hall, he thought confusedly—it must have come from the hall. He ran out there, but it was empty and quiet, and he dared not go farther away from the girl. He was supposed to watch her, and she needed watching. Claude hadn't been exaggerating the danger after all.

His cheek was not bleeding badly, and he put a handkerchief against it and called uncertainly. "Claude!"

"I thought you were going to help me," Diana said from behind him. "What's the matter with your face? What happened?"

She sensed his confusion and excitement, and he tried to pull himself together and reassure her. "It's nothing. I have a toothache."

Claude appeared from the back of the house carrying a bowl of ice and grumbling. "Why the hell is that damned woman never around? It's always her day off. No matter what day I happen to come home, it's her day off."

"Here, give me the ice." Diana took the bowl and went back to her cocktails.

Henry removed the handkerchief from his cheek and muttered, "Look. Bullet. Stay here with her. I want to search the house."

Claude's eyes bulged and he jammed his hands into his pockets to hide the fact that they were shaking. After a moment's silence he said jerkily, "Don't be a fool. You might find what you're looking for, and you're not armed. I'm going to call the police. You stay with her, and for God's sake keep your eyes open." He went upstairs, grunting at each step, presumably to use an extension phone where Diana would not hear him.

Henry turned back into the living room, and the girl called, "Come on, Papa, the cocktails are ready, and I haven't much time left."

"He went upstairs. He'll be back in a minute."

She made an exasperated little face. "He always does that. Waits until everything is ready and then disappears. Look, what makes you think that handkerchief is going to help your toothache?"

"Toothache?" Henry repeated abstractedly. "Oh. I—as a matter of fact, I scratched a pimple and drew blood."

He took a swallow of his drink and went uneasily back to the hall again. Claude should never have gone upstairs. It was dangerous. Whoever had fired that bullet might have slipped out the front door, but there had been no sound of it, and since Claude had been in the kitchen, the intruder must have gone upstairs. Aside from a soundless exit out the front door there was nothing else for him to have done. Henry took a step toward the door and then stopped. He had wanted to see whether it could be opened quietly, but he decided not to touch the handle, since the police might want to take fingerprints.

Claude came heavily down the stairs and said in a coarse whisper, "They're coming right around. You get her out of here and into that hospital."

"You'd better not stay here alone," Henry muttered, his eyes straying to the top of the stairs.

Claude displayed a small automatic and dropped it back into his pocket. "I can look after myself, but I knew he'd be gunning for that poor, innocent kid. He knows how I feel about her. She was in the office when he came whining around there, trying to get me to take his case."

"Will you two stop telling secrets in the hall?" Diana called. "It's not much fun having my farewell drink alone."

They went in to her, and Henry managed to indicate the bullet hole in the wall. Claude gave it a quick, sharp look and then sat down beside the girl and chatted to her as though he hadn't a care in the world. When she had finished her drink, she stood up and announced that she was going upstairs for her suitcase and to powder her nose.

They went with her, Claude in front and Henry behind, and while she put on her coat and hat, Claude moved restlessly, trying to curb his impatience.

As she turned from the mirror he said heartily, "You'd better be off now, dear, since you insist on going. I'll call a cab."

She pulled on her gloves and shook her head at him. "Don't bother, Papa, I can pick one up outside just as quickly."

"Yes, yes, I suppose so. I'll be around there myself as soon as I can manage it. I've a few things that must be done first. But Henry will go with you."

Diana kissed him affectionately. "Honestly, darling, I don't see why Mother couldn't get along with you. She said you were awful, you know."

Claude laughed and patted her back. "Just so long as you don't think I'm awful, baby."

Diana laughed, too, and Henry produced a false "Heh, heh."

Diana observed, "You'd better watch out for that pimple," and they all started down the stairs.

In the lower hall, before Henry could stop him, Claude opened the front door and ruined whatever fingerprints might have been on the handle. They hailed a taxi, and as it drew away from the curb Henry saw a police car stop in front of the house. Diana seemed to be looking at it, and Henry said hastily and loudly, "Will you have a cigarette?"

She held up one that was smoking between her gloved fingers. "I'm cutting down. Smoke only one cigarette at a time these days."

Henry blushed and muttered, "Sorry, I didn't see it."

"Why don't you take that handkerchief away from your face? You look silly."

"No doubt," Henry replied coldly. "I don't want the broken pimple to catch cold."

When they arrived at the hospital, Henry found some difficulty in handling the suitcase, keeping the handkerchief against his face, and paying the bill, so Diana took the suitcase. "Just so long as you pay the taxi," she said kindly. "That's all I really care about."

Henry stood beside her in the lobby while she made her arrangements. He jotted down the number of her room, and after she had disappeared into an elevator with a nurse at her elbow, he went to a phone booth and called Ted.

Ted was feeling pleased with himself. He said jauntily, "Well, I've done the impossible. You're in."

"Good. What's the number of my room?"

"For God's sake, how do I know? Who do you think you are, anyway? I hope it's a slab in the morgue."

"You keep a civil tongue in your head," Henry said austerely, "or I'll hold your bill up for months. I understand that a doctor can't stoop to the point of suing."

"You try holding my bill up for months and you'll see how far I'll stoop. Listen, when you go in—and you should go right away, in your condition—bend over forward, will you?"

"Why?"

"Never mind why," said Ted. "You're not supposed to know. Just you bend over forward."

"Shall I powder my face and draw black rings under my eyes?" Henry asked, anxious to be cooperative.

"No, the nurse would wash it off. Leave your fat, ugly face the way it is."

This reminded Henry of his cheek, and he said urgently, "You'd better come right over to the hospital. I have a wound on my face, and I want you to fix it up."

"Nuts!" Ted said cheerfully. "I have a date with a girl. Get one of the nurses to put a bandage on it."

Henry protested into a blank phone for a while, until he realized that Ted had hung up. He left the booth, bending over forward, and approached the desk with a grave look on his face. The woman behind it was staring at him, and he wondered whether she remembered him when he had escorted Diana in a completely upright position. He hoped that whatever Ted had invented for him would not keep him bent over for any great length of time.

By the time he got to his room his back was aching from the continued stooping, but he was relieved to find that it was a private room, and pleasant, and he enjoyed the thought that Claude would have to pay through the nose for it. The room was on the fourth floor, and he knew that Diana was on the fifth, which was awkward. He half considered phoning Ted again and asking for a transfer, but prudence decided him against it. Even if Ted could manage a, change, he wouldn't, in his present frame of mind. And, after all, there must be a quiet flight of stairs somewhere between the two floors.

A nurse came purposefully into the room and raised her eyebrows at him. "Not in bed yet? Here, I'll help you."

"I'm not going to bed yet," Henry said firmly.

She advanced on him. "Oh yes, you are. Naughty."

Henry looked at her carefully. She was a big woman, and determined.

"Well," he said mildly, "my suitcase hasn't arrived yet, so I have no pajamas. I'll wait until it comes."

"You don't need pajamas," the woman said, with gruesome playfulness. "I'll bring you a gown. You start undressing. I'll be right back."

Henry followed her uneasily to the door, and as soon as he saw her disappear into some sort of closet he sped down the hall and climbed the stairs to the fifth floor. He found the number of Diana's room after a certain amount of furtive peering and went in without knocking. He was pushed out immediately by an indignant nurse, who said hotly, "The young lady is undressing."

Henry said, "Oh," abstractedly, and looked at the nurse, who was young and pretty. He added, "Could you put a bandage on this for me?" and took the handkerchief away from his face.

The nurse exclaimed, "Well, I declare! What in the world happened to you?"

She led him to a sink that niched into the wall halfway up the corridor and rubbed something onto his wound with cotton batting. It smarted badly, but before he could protest she smacked a large piece of adhesive over the area, smiled at him, and went back to Diana's room on brisk, rubber-soled feet.

Henry, conscious of a stationary body beside him, turned and beheld a short, fat man who seemed to be almost entirely hairless. The fat man, looking at him with squinted eyes, said suddenly, "I want to see that," and, stretching a hand, ripped the adhesive painfully from Henry's face.

Chapter 4

"WHAT THE HELL do you think you're doing?" Henry said furiously and snatched the bandage away from the hairless man, who was peering intently at the wound on his cheek.

The man raised his voice a trifle and said, "Nurse."

One appeared immediately, and he indicated Henry with an indifferent gesture. "Fix up this man's face."

"But I just did," the nurse declared, and looked at Henry, who was trying to restore the bandage and cursing quietly because the wound had started to ooze blood again.

"Do it again," the man ordered curtly. "I'm Gilling of the police, and I'll be around for a few days." He flicked a glance at Henry and added, "You'll be all right, Mr. Debbon, just take it easy. You're lucky it only grazed your face."

The nurse led Henry to the sink again and asked with alert curiosity, "What only grazed him?"

"You attend to your own affairs, young lady," Gilling said repressively. "Are you staying here, Mr. Debbon?"

"Why should I," Henry snarled, "with a smart guy like you around?"

"I won't be around all the time, but that's between you and Mr. Boster."

Gilling walked off, and the nurse gave Henry's face a little pat. "There, I guess you'll be all right now."

Henry said "Thanks" and went back to Diana's room, with the nurse tripping along behind him. Diana was in bed, wearing a delicate pale green bed jacket and with her hair spraying in a soft red cloud over the pillow. Claude was seated in an armchair by the window, and he raised his eyebrows at Henry, who gave him a sulky frown.

Diana giggled. "You're taking that pimple too seriously, putting a whacking great bandage like that on it."

Claude stood up abruptly. "Come on out into the hall, boy, I want to talk to you." He smiled affectionately at Diana and explained, "Business, my dear. It won't take a minute."

He pushed Henry out into the hall, and the nurse had to go, too, since she was directly behind him. Claude lowered his voice and asked urgently, "Did you get in here?" and then noticed that the nurse was still with them. "That will be all, girl," he said coldly. "Go about your duties."

"If you will keep out of my way for exactly two minutes by the clock," she retorted bitterly, "maybe I can get something done."

Claude glared at her, and she swished into Diana's room with her nose in the air.

Henry touched his bandage carefully. "I'm in all right, and don't think it was easy, either. But I don't see why that plucked-looking policeman and I should both hang around."

"I can't trust him. I can't trust the police," Claude declared agitatedly. "You said you'd do the job. You *must* stay and take care of her."

"She's safe in here. For God's sake, how could the fellow get in here?"

"There are a hundred ways that he could get in, and you know it. It's worse here than at home. Come on, now, give me your room number so I can find you when I need you."

"What in hell do you want my room number for?" Henry demanded, in complete exasperation. "If I'm doing the damn lousy job I won't be there, anyway. I'll be here. It's 409, but I want to try and get it changed up to this floor."

"Four oh nine," said the voice of Gilling behind them, and they turned in time to see him writing it in a small black notebook. He snapped it shut and looked up at them. "I'll be off now."

Henry muttered, "Good!" but Gilling went on smoothly, "Between the two of you, you'd better not leave her alone for a minute, although I don't think it will take us long to pick him up. He's well marked, so it should be easy."

Claude nodded. "Right, Gilling, we'll look out for her. But I wish to God you fellas would hurry it up. There won't be any peace for me till you've got him."

Gilling walked off with his odd, straight-backed strut, and Henry sent a sneering look after him that he had to relax immediately, as it hurt his cheek.

"Now then," Claude said briskly, "my idea is that you keep watch half the time and I'll take the other half, and whichever one is off duty can sleep in your room."

Henry brightened a little. "Good! I was beginning to think this was a twenty-four-hour assignment."

"Certainly not. Do you want to take the first watch?"

Henry shook his head. "I still have to get into bed down there and show myself to the nurse. She was getting me a nightshirt, the last I heard. When you come down, you'll have to slip in while they're not looking or we'll both be thrown out. I think they're a bit short of beds here."

"I found that out," Claude said gloomily. "I tried to get a room next to my girl, and they said they wouldn't even give me a bed in the basement."

"Well"—Henry ran a finger around the edge of his collar—"of course you have to know the right people to be able to get in."

"Don't try and give me that stuff," Claude said indignantly. "I know you must have faked some sort of illness to get in, and not that scratch on your silly face, either."

"My silly face undoubtedly saved your daughter."

"O.K., O.K., but I see no reason for you to go around patting your back because your face happened to be in the way."

"I'm going down to my room," Henry said coldly. "I expect they're looking for me."

"All right. I figured we'd do four hours on and four hours off. It's five now, so you be back promptly at nine."

Henry walked down the stairs, fuming quietly all the way. Claude always wanted to run every show, and run it single-handed, giving out orders for the spadework right and left. It would be an exquisite pleasure to resign now, but of course it would also be an exquisite pleasure, and more profitable, to be a partner in the firm. Oh, well, they should be sending up supper trays soon. They always fed you at an infernally early hour in these places.

Near the door of his room he was suddenly seized and practically thrown inside. He recovered himself and swung around furiously, only to confront the large, determined nurse who had gone to get him a gown. She stood just inside the door with her arms folded and said tersely, "Get undressed."

He regarded her uncertainly and, not liking the look in her eye, was reminded of Ted's instructions and slowly sagged forward.

"And don't pretend that you can't," said the nurse, "because I have spoken to your doctor, and he says you are perfectly capable."

"Certainly. Of course I can undress myself," Henry said stiffly, "but not in front of you. If you'll just go out—"

"Oh, no." She shook her capped head firmly. "You ran out on me once, but this time I'm going to see to it that you get into bed where you belong. There's your gown, on the back of the chair."

"Look," Henry said desperately, "suppose we compromise. You turn your face to the wall, and no peeking, and I'll get out of my clothes and into that peculiar-looking garment."

She nodded and turned around. "Get going. I'll give you exactly two minutes."

Henry got going and eventually scrambled frantically into the bed, because the gown turned out to be entirely too short. He mentioned this aggrievedly, but the nurse merely said, "Nonsense," and began to move swiftly around the room, putting his clothes away and thumping a pitcher of ice water and a glass onto a small tray on the bedside table. She pinned the cord that was attached to his signal-light switch onto his pillow and passed the remark that her name was Mae, spelled M-a-e.

"I prefer to call you May, spelled M-a-y," Henry said, looking beyond her out into the corridor, where several young women were now hurrying up and down with loaded trays.

"I always tell my patients my first name," Mae explained, lowering the window a little from the top. "People never remember second names, and I don't care to be called 'Nurse,' or 'Hey, you,' but Mae. Well, people can remember that. The supe doesn't like it, of course, but when did she ever like anything except her three squares and her paycheck?"

A cheerful young woman appeared bearing a tray and, after setting it across Henry's knees, wound the back of the bed up so high that he was bent nearly double. She and Mae departed together, and Henry, after fighting off the pillows that were tumbling over his head, inspected the tray with interest.

He was immediately and violently disappointed. He switched on his signal light and waited, fuming, until Mae appeared at the door. She asked impatiently, "What is it now?"

"They've given me somebody's special diet by mistake."

Mae advanced a step and flicked her eyes over the tray. "Who sez so?"

"I say so, dammit. I'm hungry, and I want my dinner."

"That," said Mae, "is all the dinner you're going to get. You're in a hospital, handsome, and people don't eat so much here. They're too sick. When you're finished with that, you're through till breakfast, so make the most of it."

She departed quietly on her efficient white shoes, and Henry gloomily cleared the tray in three or four bites. He decided to get something more later, just before he was due to relieve Claude at nine, and to try to get some sleep in the meantime. There must be more food somewhere in this huge building, even if he had to bribe someone with Claude's money

He drifted into a pleasant sleep and was rudely awakened some time later by Gilling's impersonal voice calling his name over and over again.

"What the devil do you want?" Henry groaned. "Here I am, wounded, and so ill that I hang over forward, and people won't let me sleep in peace."

"Well," Gilling said mildly, "I thought perhaps you'd want to know. Someone has given your girlfriend a heavy dose of sleep."

Chapter 5

"WHAT IS IT?" Henry said stupidly. "Girlfriend? What do you mean?"

"The Herron girl. The nurses are running around in a dither denying singly and in chorus that they made any mistake about her medicine. They called in her doctor."

"What did he say?" Henry asked, still feeling misty with sleep.

"Says she's all right. He blames the nurses. Claims he didn't order any sort of sedative. Anyway, she's just sleeping heavy, not in any danger."

Henry rumpled his hair and asked for a cigarette. His own were in his coat pocket, but he did not want to get out of bed and let Gilling view him in the ridiculous hospital nightshirt. Gilling said he didn't have any and appeared to fall into deep thought.

Henry watched him with growing dislike. "Do you think the nurses made a mistake?" he asked presently.

"No."

"Then who do you think did it?"

"I was wondering," said Gilling composedly, "if it was you."

"Oh. Were you, indeed? And can you, for God's sake, give me any conceivable reason why I would?"

"No."

"Then why the hell do you accuse me of it?"

"I didn't accuse you. I merely said I wondered."

"I wish you'd go and wonder somewhere else," Henry said sulkily. "I'm trying to get some sleep. I didn't give the infernal girl so much as an aspirin."

"I can't see why her father would give it to her," Gilling murmured thoughtfully, "and you and he are the only ones who have been in there."

"Except you."

"Yeah," said Gilling, "except me. I wonder if I gave it to her."

"Ah, shaddup," Henry snarled. "Go and do something important, like finding this Scrimmer, for instance."

"Oh yes—Scrimmer."

"That's what I said. But you couldn't even find Evans." Gilling took out a cigarette and lit it, and Henry said in a voice of outrage, "I thought you didn't have any cigarettes."

"I didn't have one for you. Who's Evans?"

"He's disappeared," Henry said nastily, "and I'd go to the police if I were you. Be sure to ask for Gilling. He can even find things like the day you lose when you cross the equator."

"Depends on your direction." Gilling swung one leg over the other and added, "I'll give you a cigarette if you'll tell me all about Evans."

Henry flung himself out of bed, losing his sense of modesty along with his temper. He wrenched open the door of the closet and was astounded to find that his clothes had disappeared. He got into bed again and furiously jabbed at his signal light.

"Chances are they won't answer that for some time," Gilling said calmly.

Henry realized that this was all too true and gave up with bad grace. He accepted a cigarette and grudgingly told the story of Evans's disappearance. Gilling listened in silence and at the conclusion of the tale nodded briefly and departed without further comment.

Henry sat smoking his cigarette and moodily reflecting upon things that he might have said to Gilling if only he'd thought of them in time.

A nurse walked briskly into the room and asked, "Yes? What is it?"

Henry saw that it was Mae and had a hard time meeting her aggressive eye. He said shortly, "Get my clothes."

"Why? Where do you think you're going?"

"Never mind where I'm damned well going!" Henry shouted. "You bring me my clothes, and bring them in a hurry. And don't take them out of here again."

Mae stood her ground without any sign of wilting or apology. She merely gave a nasty chuckle. "You're not running out on me again, brother, and don't you think it. It doesn't look so good for a nurse if she can't keep her patients in bed where they belong. And I'm a good nurse, as anyone can tell you if you care to ask. I have your doctor's permission to keep your clothes where you can't get them, and you're staying in that bed until he discharges you."

Henry was somewhat taken aback. He had never been a patient in a hospital before, and he felt trapped and imprisoned. There were a few remarks he wanted to make to Ted, but he stored them away in his mind to be sorted out later.

He looked up at the now retreating white back and said almost humbly, "Mae."

She turned with raised eyebrows. "Well?"

"Would you be good enough to bring me the packet of cigarettes from my coat pocket?"

Mae became more friendly at once. "Sure. See, if people treat me right, I'll go to plenty of trouble to make them comfortable, but you'll soon learn you can't get anything by shouting."

"I've learned it already." Henry sighed.

"Good."

She departed, and Henry got quietly out of bed and hurried to the door. He peered out and saw her walk down the corridor some distance to a door on the opposite side, and his heart sank. It was beyond the desk, where several nurses were congregated. There was no hope of getting past them without being seen. He wondered moodily whether the desk was always draped with nurses, and if so, why it was that you always had to wait so long before one of them answered your light.

One of the nurses glanced in his direction, and he retreated into his room. He looked at his watch and thought uneasily that Claude was going to be sore—good and sore—since it was already ten minutes past nine. He heard Mae's returning footsteps and hastily climbed back in bed.

She came in wearing a cheerful smile and handed him the cigarettes, and then proceeded to hold a light and provide him with an ashtray. In his chastened mood he offered her one, but she shook her head.

"See, I'm not allowed to smoke on duty, but I'll just take a puff of yours, if you don't mind."

He did mind, but he held the smoking cylinder out to her in silence. She inhaled expertly and then busied herself around the room doing nothing, coming back at intervals for another puff. When the cigarette had disappeared, in short order, Mae asked him if he'd like another.

"No, thank you," Henry said courteously. "I think I'll try and sleep now."

Mae said, "Sure," and with a few swift movements had him lying flat on a vigorously shaken pillow, the light out, the window open, and the door shut with herself outside.

"She didn't kiss me good night," Henry said into the empty darkness.

He got out of bed and went to the door, which he opened a crack. Several nurses were still clustered around the desk, and he wondered despairingly how he was going to get his clothes. He paced the room, conscious of chill on the bare parts of him that were accustomed to being covered, until he stubbed his toe. He cursed fluently but quietly until an idea slid into his mind. There was a man in the next room—he'd caught a glimpse of him—and presumably the man had clothes. Also, presumably he was a tractable patient, so that his clothes were doubtless hanging in his closet.

The thing was accomplished with surprising ease. He slipped into the next room while the nurses had their heads bent over something on the desk, and there was no move from the sleeping figure on the bed. Probably, Henry thought, the fellow had had a pill of some sort. He found clothes hanging in the closet, and although it was not easy getting into the trousers in the dark, he managed it without making any noise. The shoes seemed to push his feet out sideways and the trousers were very roomy, but he belted them tightly. At least he was clothed. He still wore the hospital nightshirt on the upper part of his body, and he hoped that it would make him look like an intern or an orderly.

He slipped out into the hall and made his way toward the stairs, away from the desk. He could not keep his back from prickling at the thought that Mae's eyes might alight on it, but he made the stairs without trouble. He tightened the other man's belt again and smoothed his hair. Luckily, Diana's room was near the head of the stairs, and he made it without anyone having seen him at all.

He opened the door quietly and went in, fully expecting a blast of abuse from Claude, and was astonished to find that Claude was not there. He went to the foot of the bed and saw that Diana was sleeping quietly. He turned away, and at the same time heard a pinging sound that sent his heart pounding into his throat.

He raised a shaking finger and touched a fresh bullet hole in the wall.

Chapter 6

HENRY SWUNG around and started across the room, and at the same time Claude emerged from another door. Henry looked at him only long enough to establish his identity and then plunged out into the hall. He looked wildly up and down, but there was no one in sight, and after a moment's hesitation he hurried to the head of the stairs. He looked down into emptiness but decided uneasily that someone could have escaped this way, since the stairs were fairly close to Diana's room and it had taken him a few shocked moments to start his pursuit. He walked slowly back to the room, where he found Claude standing in the doorway exhibiting signs of rage.

"What the damn is the matter with you?" he demanded in a hoarse whisper. "What are you running all over the place dressed like a ruddy clown for?"

Henry looked down at himself and was conscious of a moment's shame. There was room, far too much room, in the width of the trousers, but they ended about halfway down his calf, and the saddle shoes were a dirty and scuffed black and white. He felt a spasm of illogical annoyance at the owner of these garments, but it faded away as he remembered the bullet hole. He pushed into Diana's room and Claude followed, still rumbling angrily. Claude had now got to the burning question of why Henry was so late.

They arrived together at the bullet hole in the wall, and Claude stopped speaking abruptly while they examined it.

"It came from the hall door," Henry said in a low voice. "I'm sure of it. What's that other door, the one you came through?"

"Bathroom, you idiot," Claude whispered furiously.

Henry walked over and opened the bathroom door. There was a faint, feminine scream, and he shut it again immediately, his face reddening.

"Why didn't you tell me it might be in use?" he demanded fiercely.

"Because it has no Goddamned right to be in use!" Claude hissed, his face purple. "I bought that bathroom for Diana—it's hers—and that connecting door damned well ought to be locked on this side." He put an angry thumb on the signal button that was tucked in beside his sleeping daughter and muttered, "We'll see about this." He punched the button violently several times and whispered to Henry. "You can see that we've got to get her out of here. She isn't safe. He's a killer, and I knew the murdering louse would get in here somehow. We've got to get her out right away."

"The door was open when I came in," Henry said. "Why didn't you keep it shut?"

"I did keep it shut, but you can't lock them, and the blasted nurse keeps coming in."

"You'd better go out and get a nurse or someone to call the police," Henry said abruptly. "He can't be very far away yet."

Claude nodded and began to move toward the door. "The damned Gilling fella has been snooping around underfoot all evening until I need him, and then he goes off. Probably sitting in a poker game waiting for the ruddy murderer to walk up to him and hold out his hands."

He went along to the desk where a clean-looking nurse was busily writing and said peremptorily, "Get me the downstairs switchboard."

She looked up at him. "Visiting hours are over."

Claude bared his teeth and spoke through them. "I don't give a curse for your stupid little visiting hours. Who said anything about visiting? I want the downstairs switchboard."

"What for? To play with? They need it themselves."

"Yes," said Claude, with sudden deadly calm, "they probably do, so don't bother them. You'll just have to think up some other way to get in touch with the police. Maybe you could lean out the window and yell."

The nurse immediately and efficiently telephoned the main switchboard and requested that someone, whose name eluded Claude, be sent up to the fifth floor without delay, after which she smiled up at Claude and asked cheerfully, "Having a little trouble?"

Claude, still deadly calm but still speaking through his bared teeth, said, "Yes, since you mention it, I am having a little trouble. Nothing much, of course. I merely wished the police to catch a murderer, but, naturally, hospital red tape insures his having plenty of time to get away. It is probably just as well. No doubt the poor fella never meant any harm—early childhood influences, perhaps. If he happens to be hiding on this floor, lurking in some dark corner, ready to pounce, be sure to tell him before he smashes your pretty little cap into your dumb little head that visiting hours are over."

He turned on his heel and went back to Diana's room, where he found Henry standing in the doorway.

"Nice to see you watching over her so closely," he said, in the same voice he had used to the nurse.

Henry raised his eyebrows. "I found her entirely alone when I came on the job."

"For God's sake!" Claude raved. "Do you think I'm a blasted ruddy camel? I was in the bathroom for maybe two minutes."

"You should have closed the door and pushed the bureau in front of it," Henry said, enjoying himself.

There was a step behind them, and they both started and swung around.

"Take it easy, boys—no bloodshed," Gilling said unemotionally.

"Why the hell don't you knock when you come in here?" Claude demanded furiously.

"Scrimmer wouldn't knock. You should watch out for that sort of thing. Look how easily I crept up behind you."

Henry exhibited the bullet hole, and Gilling began to question them, quietly and thoroughly. If an answer were not satisfactory, he had no hesitation about repeating himself, and at last Claude burst out, "Good God! D'ya think I look at my watch every time I go to let nature take its course?"

"At your age," said Gilling calmly, "it would not be a bad idea. Now—"

"Oh, get out of here!" Claude moaned, in a sort of whispered howl. "Get the hell out of here and go and catch Scrimmer. You should have picked him up long ago. He's probably thumbing his nose at the entire fat-headed police force."

Gilling nodded without any loss of aplomb. "No doubt. He's the vulgar type, you know. Anyway, he seems to have disappeared off the face of the earth. So has Evans. Have you any idea where Evans is, Mr. Boster?"

"For Chrissake!" Claude muttered, astounded. "Do you mean to tell me you're wasting time looking for Evans? He's in my office. He'll be in my office until the trumpet blows, except for intervals of eating and sleeping. And when he has to go—and even Evans has to go—I'll bet he *does* look at his watch. Now, get going, will you, and find that murdering devil. I've twice nearly lost a valuable employee because of your fumbling."

Henry threw back his shoulders, and Gilling glanced at him. "Would you mind telling me what kind of a costume that is you're wearing, Mr. Debbon?"

"Not at all," Henry said coldly. "It's my slack suit. I've been meaning to ask you, since you're around here so much, if you'd bring me some things from my hotel room. I'll give you a list and the key."

To Henry's surprise, Gilling dispensed with the sarcasm entirely and merely said, "Be glad to." He produced a notebook and pencil and waited for the list. Henry gave it to him and added a note for the hotel asking that Gilling be allowed into his room, since he did not have his key. Gilling offered to wait while he went downstairs and got the key, but Henry explained that owing to a temperamental nurse it was not readily available.

Claude and Gilling went off, Gilling presumably to continue the hunt for Scrimmer and Claude to find room 409, enter it without being seen by any of the nurses, and try to get some sleep.

Henry closed Diana's door and pushed the bureau across in front of it. It made a loud squeaking noise and cut a long, jagged hole in the linoleum, but he was too tired to care. He slumped into the armchair and lit a cigarette, then glanced at the bed. Diana's eyes were open, and she was staring at him.

"You awake?" he muttered, startled.

She raised herself in the bed and said shrilly, "What is it? What do you want?"

"Nothing, nothing," Henry replied hastily. "I—I'm just visiting."

"Those clothes—do you usually visit dressed like that? And why is the bureau in front of the door?"

"Oh—I—these clothes." Henry looked down at them and produced a croaking laugh. "I'm in for a checkup, and the nurse mislaid my clothes. I was bored down there in my room, so I borrowed these things to come up and see you."

She looked at him for a long minute, and then whispered, "The bureau?"

"The—oh, yes—the bureau. There's a—a mental patient wandering around. Makes me nervous."

She struggled higher in the bed, and her eyes looked dark and enormous. "I don't believe you."

Henry lapsed into an uneasy silence. How could he tell the girl that Scrimmer had twice tried to take her life? Twice two bad shots.

Henry suddenly tensed in his chair and drew a gasping breath. Scrimmer hadn't been aiming at Diana. He was trying to kill Henry Debbon.

Chapter 7

HENRY SWALLOWED and felt himself turning pale. Diana said, "You'd better move that bureau away. I've already put my light on, and the nurse will be here any minute."

Henry pushed the bureau back to its original position and turned to the girl rather desperately. "Don't tell the nurse anything, or your father will be furious. You know very well that I'm here under his orders. He made me come here tonight when he left. You'd better talk to him before you start anything."

He heard the nurse at the door and slipped into the bathroom and then was astounded to hear Diana say to her, "There's some sort of crazy man in a queer costume who's been bothering me. He went into the bathroom."

Henry retreated quietly from the bathroom into the room that connected with it on the other side. It was quite dark, and as far as he could make out the woman in the bed was sleeping quietly. He fumbled around until he found the closet and then slipped in, leaving the door a little ajar. He heard the nurse walk through the bathroom, and after a moment she opened the door and looked into the dark room beyond, but she did not come in. She closed the bathroom door and locked it, and he heard her say to Diana, "Did you know this door was unlocked? It shouldn't be. This is your bathroom. Somebody was careless. But anyway, dear, there's no one around here." Her voice became fainter as she returned to Diana's room. "You know you had a pill by mistake, so you're pretty sleepy. In fact, you shouldn't be awake at all right now."

"You mean you didn't find him?" Diana's voice was shrill and therefore clearer. "But he hangs around all the time, and I don't want him here any more."

"You were dreaming, dear," the nurse said, in the voice of one who has already started to think about something else. "Those pills are apt to give you queer dreams."

"I was *not* dreaming," Diana declared indignantly, "and I want you to find that man and take him away."

"All right, dear," the nurse murmured soothingly. "You just go back to sleep now, and I'll attend to everything."

She straightened the bed, punched and reversed the pillow, and left the room, switching off the light as she went. Diana wanted to sit up and put the light on again. Surely that man Henry must be quite mad. He looked like it and he acted like it, but the drug she'd had was too much for her, and she drifted off to sleep despite herself.

Henry was obliged to enter her room by way of the hall. There were not many people around at that time, and he was able to manage it without being seen, but he was vastly relieved to find Diana asleep. He did not close the door this time, but sat in the darkened room and watched the bar of light that shone in from the hall. The door was only partially ajar, and he and Diana were both behind it, so that he felt reasonably safe.

He sat back and lit a cigarette and then realized that he was hungry. He hadn't had dinner—you couldn't call those few scraps on the tray a meal—and he felt that he'd like to eat well and fully before he was fired on again. Third time for luck. The first time he'd been standing at Diana's right, and the bullet grazed his right cheek—rotten shot, if the fellow had been aiming at her. The second bullet had come from the door leading to the hall—an even worse effort, if it were the girl he was after—and so it wasn't the girl, but Henry himself. All done with some sort of a silencer too—no noise. Henry moved his cramped body and frowned into the darkness. If Claude had any conscience at all, he'd make him a partner right now, after putting him into such a dangerous position.

The thing didn't actually make sense, Henry thought uneasily. Why would anyone want to shoot him? Unless, of course, Scrimmer thought he was Claude's stupid son Fred. And that was it. That must be it. Henry sagged forward once more, but this time in real pain at the idea that he might have to die in Fred's place.

He'd have to do something. He couldn't just sit here and take it— give up his life for nothing. He got up and began to pace the room restlessly. The girl was probably safe enough, so why didn't he just go down and explain everything to Claude and walk out on the job? That's what he ought to do, and yet he couldn't. Scrimmer might come back, find the girl alone, and decide that since he hadn't been able to get Fred, he might as well settle for her. The man must be pretty desperate for revenge when he took a chance on hanging around with the entire police force out looking for him.

Henry sat down again and pulled out his cigarettes from the pocket of the brief and bulging trousers. Damn it, he'd have to get his own clothes. Somehow, he'd have to manage it. He found that he had no matches and went over to the bedside table, where he fumbled around unsuccessfully for a while before returning gloomily to his chair. The whole thing was screwy, he thought peevishly. A hardened criminal like this Scrimmer wouldn't hang around so dangerously. His immediate concern would be to escape completely. He could always wait until things had died down and then come back and get even with Claude later.

Henry got up again. He'd have to find a match somewhere. He wanted a smoke. He tried the bedside table again without result and then thought of the room on the other side of the bathroom. Perhaps the woman in there was a smoker and had left matches around.

He went quietly through the bathroom and unlocked the farther door. It would not open at first, and at last he gave a mighty tug, and it flew back and hit him on the chin. He subdued a desire to wrench it from its hinges and went into the darkened room, where the woman still seemed to be sleeping heavily. He found cigarettes and matches almost immediately and decided to take them all, since it seemed obvious that his need was more acute than hers. Someone could bring her cigarettes in the morning, and anyway, too much smoking wasn't good for her, ill as she must be.

He began to feel his way back to the bathroom and suddenly stopped short. There was something there. Some darker mass that was out of place. Something that should have been the bathroom door and was not. It was Scrimmer, Henry thought instantly, and was surprised at his own coolness. Scrimmer waiting for him to pass, so that he could get rid of another bullet.

Henry backed up silently and moved sideways toward the hall door. It was closed. The man had probably closed it when he came in, and that was why the room was so dark. He opened it and slid out in one motion and then stood for a moment looking up and down the hall. There was a nurse down at the end of the corridor, but she was not looking at him, and he went quickly back to Diana's room. He switched on the light, padded across to the bathroom door, and opened it cautiously. There was no sound, so he switched on the light in there, went swiftly to the farther door, and carefully locked it. He tried it twice to make sure that there was no mistake and then hurried back to the bedroom, where he closed the hall door and stood leaning against it, wiping the moisture from his brow.

When he had recovered himself a little, he swung the bureau across in front of the door, more quietly this time, and took the precaution of moving Diana's signal-light switch out of her reach.

He sat down rather heavily in the armchair and pulled out a cigarette. Where the devil was that smug, strutting little jerk Gilling? Never around when you wanted him. Could it have been that woman patient in there, huddling against the bathroom door because she'd heard him in her room? No, that was out. She'd have screamed. And anyway, he'd heard her breathing on the bed. Maybe it was Gilling doing a little private spying. And maybe not. Gilling was doubtless at home in bed with his fat head on a pillow, getting his eight hours.

Who was this Scrimmer, anyhow? Pitty, Claude had called him. Why Pitty? Was that Mrs. Scrimmer's bright idea of a name for the baby?

Henry suddenly tensed, and a piece of hot ash fell onto his ankle. Oh no. The name Pitty had come later, after little Scrimmer's smooth face had become pockmarked—pitted. That's who he was—the pockmarked man who had come into Claude's office so early in the morning.

Chapter 8

HENRY THOUGHT about the pockmarked man, who must certainly be Pitty Scrimmer. He had gone into Claude's office, but he hadn't taken a shot at Claude. He simply had not been there when Claude went in. He must have been hiding in the closet then, and he'd waited until they'd all gone out for coffee before he left. Perhaps he'd taken Evans along with him.

Henry shook his head impatiently. The whole thing was absurd. He glanced up as the bed light went on and saw that Diana was frantically looking for her signal switch. She appeared to be terrified, and he said hastily, "Please, there's no reason to be afraid. If you'll just listen to me for a moment I'll explain."

She whispered, "Go away. Go and get Papa for me. Get him right away."

"Papa," said Henry, "is sleeping downstairs in a room we managed to wangle. We're taking turns looking after you because he thinks your life is in danger. As a matter of fact, I don't think you're in any danger at all, so there's no reason for you to be scared."

The only answer she gave him was to open her mouth and produce a thin scream.

Henry pulled out a battered cigarette, lit it, and muttered, "Oh, what the hell!"

Diana's eyes were still huge and frightened in her white face, but she said almost steadily, "The room is blue with smoke right now."

"Somebody's burning garbage," Henry said shortly. He looked at the brand of the cigarette he had taken from the woman in the next room and amended disgustedly, "Me." There was a discreet little tap on the door, and he went over and flung the bureau away from it. Gilling slid in, shut the door behind him, and said, "Shh."

Henry regarded him coldly. "I thought you'd gone to a good movie long ago. Didn't anyone else hear her scream?"

"No," Gilling said imperturbably, "the nurse didn't even look up from her work. I heard it, of course, and I came straight down."

"They teach these cops to wash their ears every day," Henry explained to Diana, but she was looking at Gilling and ignored him entirely.

She raised shaking hands to push her hair back from her face and whispered, "Who are you?"

Gilling seemed a little surprised that he had not been explained to her and said simply, "I'm Gilling of the police."

"The police? But what is it? What's happened?" Her voice rose hysterically, and Gilling went over to her and spoke in a soothing manner.

"It's quite all right. You should really try to sleep. Shall I get a nurse?"

"Yes, yes, please call a nurse."

Gilling pretended to press the call switch and then went to the door as though he were awaiting the nurse. Diana watched him for a while, and then, in spite of herself, her heavy eyes closed, and she was asleep again.

Gilling came back from the door and said to Henry, "If you'd like to go, I shall stay here for the rest of the night."

"Wait a minute." Henry rumpled his hair fretfully. "I think there was someone in the next room, aside from the patient, I mean, trying to get in here maybe. I went through the bathroom to open the door, and it stuck."

"Doors do," Gilling said mildly. "Why did you try to open it?"

"What?"

"Why were you trying to go through? Had you heard a noise in the next room?"

"No," said Henry sulkily, "I was trying to find some matches."

"Oh, I see. Tell me."

Henry told him, and Gilling listened, if not with bated breath, at least courteously. In the end he went into the next room, while Henry waited, and eventually returned to state calmly, "No one in there now, except the patient. You may go to bed if you like."

"Why?" Henry asked aggressively.

"No necessity for both of us to be here, and I want Scrimmer to think she's alone."

Henry shrugged. "Did you bring the things from my hotel? My clothes?"

Gilling nodded towards the bureau, which was beginning to look a bit battered. "Over there."

"Good God!" Henry said, astounded. "That small package?"

"Just necessary stuff. I was unable to bring all the things you had listed."

"I haven't even a coat!" Henry protested wildly. "No coat, and I have to go out and eat. I'm starving. And no money. How can I get a decent meal with no money?"

"You did not have money on the list."

Henry put the package under his arm and flung out of the room without another word. He got downstairs and to his own room without meeting anyone and was thoroughly irritated to find Claude lying on his bed, fully dressed except for his coat, and snoring loudly. Henry woke him and took pleasure in being abrupt and rough.

Claude rolled off the bed, staggered, and muttered thickly, "What is it? What's the time?"

"Never mind the time. Gilling's with her, and he's taken over. He sent me away. But I need some money."

"For Chrissake, what do you need money for?" Claude whispered savagely. "And turn off the light. Somebody might come along."

Henry ignored him. He was opening his package, and he murmured disconsolately, "One pair of trousers, one shirt, one pair of shoes. He didn't even bring me any socks."

Claude snapped off the light, and Henry changed into his own clothes in the dark. "Where's your overcoat?" he asked in a stage whisper.

Claude got onto the bed. "I don't know, and I don't give a curse. I think I left it up in Diana's room."

"Well, give me some money, will you? They've taken all my money away."

"Oh, for God's sake!" Claude exploded. "Do you want me to wipe your nose too? Your blasted money is probably in the drawer here beside your bed. They never take money away." He jerked the drawer open, but it was too dark to see whether there was any money, and at last he pulled his wallet from his pocket and flung a bill at Henry. "Where are you going that you need money, anyway?"

Henry took the bill and explained stiffly, "I am going out to get something to eat. I'm starving."

"How do you think you're going to get out?" Claude snorted. "You're supposed to be a patient here."

Henry picked up Claude's suit coat, which was hanging over a chair, and put it on. "I shall pretend I'm an orderly. I understand it isn't so easy to get orderlies these days, and they can do pretty much as they like." He went to the mirror and tried to arrange his hair in a way that he thought an orderly would wear it, but it was too dark to see the result.

"I think you're completely nuts," Claude said from the bed. "Why don't you lie down and try to get some rest?"

"Beside you?" Henry asked coldly. "Or on the floor? Or do you think I should sit in the armchair and review my sins until morning?"

"You couldn't cover the ground by morning," Claude said nastily.

"Do what you want, but remember this. I want my coat back at one o'clock—that's when you get this bed—and in the meantime, I expect you to check on Gilling and make sure that he's still there. The Godforsaken lout should have picked up Scrimmer long ago. The whole thing is a crying scandal, and I intend to expose it."

Henry agreed only torpidly, since nothing seemed of much importance now except food. He hoped that there would be an all-night restaurant near the hospital, because he knew that he was going to be cold with no overcoat and not even an undershirt. Claude's coat was too big. He could feel drafts blowing around inside it already.

He started down the stairs and continued all the way to the bottom. He felt that his demeanor must be as one who had an object—a busy man between appointments—and then nobody would have the temerity to stop him. He reached the lobby and kept his eyes away from the sleepy-looking woman who presided behind the desk. He had an uneasy feeling that her eyes were boring into his back, but he walked purposefully to the door and went through it without having been challenged.

It was bitterly cold, and he hurried into the first eating house whose lights told him it was still operating. The place was dirty, and when he was served with food, it tasted as though it had been frying for weeks, but he was too hungry to care. He ate everything, paid for his meal with Claude's bill, and pocketed the change.

He felt a good deal better, and as he made his way back to the hospital he decided that he'd better wake Claude and tell him about Pitty Scrimmer. Explain that it must have been Scrimmer who had come into the office so early and disappeared into Claude's room.

On the hospital steps Henry stopped suddenly and forgot the cold that was numbing his whole body. There was no closet in Claude's office, he remembered. There was no place that the man could have hidden and no other exit.

Chapter 9

HENRY WENT on into the lobby of the hospital. He gave a quick side glance at the woman behind the desk and then looked straight ahead. It might be harder to get back in than it had been to get out, but what did that matter, anyway? Why did he want to get in? He should have gone straight home. Diana was all right, with Gilling hanging around. Maybe he would go home, only he'd better go up first and tell Claude he was quitting, and he'd better get there before Claude left.

In the meantime, there was that woman at the desk. He sauntered past her, looking in another direction, and forming mental answers to her possible questions. He'd tell her he was a hungry patient who'd had to go on the outside to get enough to eat.

He reached the stairs at last without her having noticed him at all as far as he could see. He was slightly bitter about it. If he'd been desperate to get past, she'd certainly have stopped him, but since he did not care much, his genuine unconcern made him inconspicuous.

He went up the stairs without meeting anyone, and when he reached his room, he found Claude pacing the floor in an explosive temper.

"Damn it to hell, where have you been with my coat?"

Henry shrugged out of it and handed it over. "I've been giving it an airing to keep the moths out. I told you I had to eat, didn't I?"

Claude jerked his arms into the coat and said peevishly, "I can't sleep on that blasted bed. I'm aching from head to foot. How the devil do they expect sick people to stand it? I'm going home. I'm no good when I don't get my sleep and as long as Gilling is with Diana, she'll be all right. You get some sleep, too, if you can sleep on that foul bed."

Henry looked fondly at the foul bed and said cheerfully, "O.K."

"But remember, you're to get up there early in the morning."

"Certainly, of course," Henry said impatiently. "Listen, before you go I want to tell you something. You know there are no hiding places in your office, and—"

"Was there a bar in that hash house you went to?" Claude demanded. "Too bad about the hiding places. I'll have some installed. I suppose you and the girls play hide and seek while I'm out working my ears off for all of you. Well, I'm off. Remember what I told you about getting up there early."

He pounded out of the room and headed for the stairs, while Henry watched him sourly. He'll be cold, he thought, without his overcoat, and serve him right. The overcoat was probably hanging in Diana's closet, and he could wear it himself when he left in the morning.

A nurse appeared from the direction of the desk, and Henry backed into the room and speedily removed his clothes. He pulled on the hospital's idea of a bed garment and scrambled in between the sheets just as the nurse came briskly into the room. She carried a flashlight which she shone directly onto his face, and Henry blinked and tried to look sleepy.

"What were you doing out of bed?" she asked sternly. "And that friend of yours who just left is entirely out of order, staying so late. Don't you know that visitors are supposed to leave at nine o'clock?"

"Yes," Henry said in a small voice, "but he wouldn't go. He was telling me how he'd put it over on a couple of other fellows in a business deal, and to be quite frank with you, I've been bored for some time."

"You had your trousers on," she said accusingly. "I saw you. Where did you think you were going?"

"I was not going," Henry retorted stiffly, "I was returning."

She gave his drawsheet a couple of sharp tugs that raised his back off the bed, adjusted the window, and said firmly, "Now you go to sleep."

She left the room, switching off her flashlight as she went, and Henry began to fumble around for a cigarette. He couldn't find one and remembered his cigarettes were in the pocket of his trousers. He decided to get one later and to do a lot of heavy thinking first. It was, in fact, the last thought he had before he went into a sound sleep.

He awoke, groaning, to find a small, cheerful nurse standing beside him, bearing a basin. She deposited the basin upon his bedside table, added towels and soap, and said chirpily, "Hiya. Wash yourself all over, like a good boy."

"This is all a waste of time," Henry said austerely. "I never wash in between times."

She put her hands on her hips, and asked, "In between what times?"

"I take a shower, not a basin, in the morning."

"Not this morning you don't," she said, still cheerful. "You're in a hospital this morning, so you take a basin. And don't forget about behind your ears."

"All right, all right," Henry said irritably, "so I'll wash with that bit of spit in the basin, but not with you here. Beat it."

Another nurse poked her head inside the door and spoke in an exasperated tone of voice. "Ruby, what's holding you up? I told you to hurry. Get out of here now. I'll finish this one."

Henry, feeling like an inanimate specimen, frowned at both of them, but they ignored him completely. Ruby departed, cheerful to the end, and the newcomer advanced on him with swishing skirts. She washed him vigorously and swiftly, ignoring all his protests. In the end she said, "That'll do for today. We're running a bit behind, and I haven't any more time. You do the rest yourself."

She was out of the room before he could reply, and he lay there, seething with indignation. Ted was responsible for this, he thought furiously. Pure malice, probably. When he had calmed down a little, he decided to do the rest himself, as bidden by the nurse. It would save him from having to take a shower, anyway. He discovered that the water in the basin was cold by now, and he finished his ablutions with assortment of muttered curses. "Just pushing the mud around from one spot to another," he said to the empty room. "No wonder people die like flies in a hospital. They simply give up with all the odds against them."

"Wot's that, sir?" a voice said amiably, and Henry dived under the bedclothes with his face glowing red. He peered out and saw a large woman wielding a mop over the floor. She smiled and nodded at him and appeared to be completely unconcerned over having seen him more or less naked.

He lay still with his eyes fixed rigidly on the ceiling, hating everything and everybody, and his mortification was enhanced by the fact that the bedclothes were now quite wet in a lot of places.

The woman departed after a short time, and Henry decided grimly that they cleaned the rooms in the same way that they cleaned the patients—sloppily.

He started to get out of bed, but had to climb back in a hurry when a young girl entered bearing his breakfast tray. She said, "Good morning," and deposited the tray across his knees, with one of the supporting legs slipping inward. Henry grasped at it as it started to sag, and the girl wound the bed up behind him until he was leaning forward. It was impossible for him to get out of bed now. He had to hang onto one end of the tray, and every time he moved, a stream of weak-looking coffee poured out of the spout of the pot. He decided, gloomily, that he might as well eat the breakfast. Certainly it wouldn't take long, for there wasn't much.

He was still hungry when he had cleared the tray, but now, at least, he could push it to the bottom of the bed without disaster and get out.

He was standing on the floor, looking vaguely around for his clothes, when Ruby walked in. He glared at her and frantically pulled his short gown down in the direction of his knees.

"Hiya," Ruby said amiably. "What are you doing out of bed? Come on in, Joe."

Joe materialized as an orderly pushing a wheelchair. He brought the chair to rest, leaned languidly on the back, and gave Henry an impersonal grin.

Ruby had opened the closet door and now asked from its depths, "Where's your robe?"

"The moths ate it," Henry said ill-temperedly. "If you'll get out, I'll put on my trousers."

"You don't want your trousers," Ruby replied sunnily. "Here, I'll fix you up. We're late now." She pushed him into the wheelchair, with Joe's help, and tucked a blanket around the blatant nakedness of his knees. "There you are—all set."

The seat of the chair was cold, and Henry tried to struggle out again, but was restrained by Joe.

"Look here—wait a minute—you've made a mistake. It's some other patient you're looking for."

Ruby and Joe appeared to have forgotten him at this point. They were exchanging items of hospital gossip, and they wheeled him out of the room and down the hall to the elevator, where Ruby left with a pert grin for each of them.

"Where the hell do you think you're taking me?" Henry bawled.

Joe said, "Quiet, Bub. What's eatin' you, anyways? They ain't gonna carve you this mornin'. This is only X-rays."

It was X-rays, and it took longer than Henry had anticipated. He was able to get two short naps during the course of the morning, but it was noon before Joe appeared to wheel him back to his room. His luncheon tray was sitting on the bed, and Joe put it on the floor, heaved him between the sheets, and then jammed the tray under his chin. He said, "There you are, Bub. Feed your face while you can. Maybe you'll be livin' on milk tomorrow, after they get through shakin' their heads over all them X-rays."

Henry ignored him and began to inhale the few dainty bits of food that decorated the tray. He was trying to get his teeth into a mouthful of junket when Claude stalked in and stood glaring at him.

"Why don't you sit down?" Henry asked sourly. "Transfer all that weight from your feet to your—"

"Go on," Claude thundered, "sit there with pillows behind you, gorge your beastly stomach on my money, while Diana has disappeared."

Chapter 10

HENRY NEARLY choked over a piece of creamed something or other, and Claude stood and watched stonily while he fought for breath. When his windpipe was clear once more Claude said coldly, "I wouldn't have cared."

"Nothing surprising about that," Henry replied, with chilly courtesy. "It's the sort of appreciation most people get when they die in the line of duty." He gulped down some coffee, and added, "Where did she go?"

"Do you think I'd be standing here chatting with an ape like you if I knew where she'd gone?" Claude howled.

Henry pushed the tray to the bottom of the bed, threw the covers aside, and carefully lowered himself to the floor.

"You're a horrible sight," Claude commented bitterly.

Henry stalked to the closet and pulled out his few clothes. He noticed uneasily that the trousers and shoes belonging to the man in the next room were still there, but he felt there was nothing he could do about it just now. He asked briefly, "Where's Gilling?"

"I don't know where Gilling is," Claude snarled, "and the way I feel about him now, I don't care."

"Do the nurses know where she went?"

"No."

"Are they looking for her?"

"Of course not," Claude said, staring at him.

"You mean a patient is missing and nobody bothers to find out where she is?"

"You," said Claude gloomily, "have a head of solid ivory. The doctor *dismissed* her—decides he doesn't want to carve her, after all—going to do something else to her nose—just like that. If I—as a blasted lawyer—changed my mind as airily as that, I'd be drummed out of business in no time."

"What's wrong with her nose?"

"Nothing. Not a ruddy thing. She never even sniffles. But these infernal pill slingers have to earn money to pay their lousy butlers."

"You mean," Henry interrupted, "that after she left the hospital, she never went home? You phoned?"

"Did you think I sent a carrier pigeon?" Claude yelled. "I phoned home, and she isn't there, and I phoned some of her friends, and she isn't there. And then I wasted a nickel phoning Gilling. He was still in bed—probably a hangover."

"Phone home again," Henry advised calmly. "Perhaps she's turned up by this time. There's a phone down the hall."

Claude pounded out of the room, and Henry went to the door and glanced up and down the hall. He caught sight of Ruby, who pattered over and said, "Hi there, where you going?"

Henry gazed at her thoughtfully for a moment and assumed a false smile. "I'm going home. Isn't that a break? The X-rays disclosed that I have no appendix, and since that was what my doctor intended to remove, he's had to give up the whole project."

She looked at him doubtfully. "Well, gee, I didn't hear anything like that."

"No, Ruby, because they're not always frank with you here. They keep things from you. Personally, I wouldn't put up with it. Would you be good enough to get my clothes? They're in that closet down the hall."

"Are those your clothes?" she asked wonderingly.

"They are, yes. The head nurse put them there because I had some visitors last night who are not entirely trustworthy."

Ruby giggled and went off in the direction of the closet, and Claude returned, mopping his damp brow.

"All right, so she's there. I suppose I'm jittery. And no wonder. She stopped to do some shopping. Anyway, we've got to get to the house right away. I can't have her there alone."

Henry, peering nervously after Ruby, said, "You mean *you* have to get to the house."

"What are you talking about?"

"Pitty Scrimmer is too bum a shot. I have one life to live, and I might as well live it."

"Actually," said Claude nastily, "there's no sense to that at all, but I suppose you're prejudiced."

Ruby came tripping back with Henry's clothes at this point and said dubiously as she handed them over, "Nobody's on the floor right now, only me. They're having lunch. You can't go till somebody comes, see, because I'm only a student—"

"Perfectly all right," Henry assured her. "Don't fail to let me know when authority arrives."

Ruby looked relieved, said, "O.K.," and flew off about her work. Henry retreated into his room and began rapidly to dress.

Claude sat down and watched him abstractedly. "Do you mean to tell me," he said presently, "that you really think you're in danger?"

"I don't know what's going on," Henry admitted, "but that man must have been in the office yesterday, and of course he saw me. Where he disappeared to I don't know. He couldn't have hidden in your office, and after you were in there, Miss Robb went in. Still and all, he went in there, he saw me, and now he wants to shoot me. And, incidentally, where's Evans?"

"Would you mind," Claude said helplessly, "telling me what in hell you're talking about?"

"Maybe you can understand this. I'm taking a few days off, and I'm going down to my place in the country."

Claude pulled out a cigar, lighted it carefully, and stared at the glowing tip in silence for a while. Presently he observed almost mildly, "You're yellow."

"I certainly am."

"What place in the country?"

Henry said, "You know very well what place in the country."

"I would hardly call it a place in the country," Claude said, "if you mean that old barn your aunt left you."

"Oh no?" Henry, retorted, stung. "It's a place, isn't it? It's in the country, isn't it?"

Claude dropped cigar ash onto the floor and stretched his fat legs. "It would give people a better idea of the property if you called it the haunted ruin."

"What's haunted about it, for God's sake?" Henry demanded belligerently.

"Noises. They go on all night long. Maybe it's because part of the house is closed up. I couldn't get rid of the idea that someone was living in there—or some *thing.*"

Henry knotted his tie savagely and maintained a haughty silence. Claude was being ridiculous, and there was no use arguing with him when he was in that mood.

He finished dressing, folded his other clothes, and took a worried look at the trousers and shoes belonging to the man next door. In the end he spread them out on his own bed, and hoped that they and their owner would somehow get together.

"It leaks, too," Claude said from his chair, "and if you try to open a window, you're bound to break a fingernail or gash your hand."

Henry peered out of the door and was relieved to find that no one was in sight. He hurried to the stairs and went down, quickly, but restrained himself from running. There were several people in the lobby, but he walked briskly through without looking at anyone and was not challenged. Someone was getting out of a cab at the door, and he slid in, leaning back against the leather with a sigh of relief. He had opened his mouth to direct the driver when someone poured into the seat beside him, and Claude's voice gave the address of Claude's house.

"Now listen—wait a minute!" Henry protested. "This is my cab— you can have it when I'm through."

"We'll all be through together." Claude mopped his glowing face and bunched the handkerchief back into his pocket. "There's plenty of room in that old house of yours. Diana and I'll come along and stay with you for a while."

"You'll do nothing of the kind," Henry yelled furiously. "You can't bring a girl out there. It's primitive. I haven't got around to fixing it up yet."

Claude extracted the bunched handkerchief and mopped his face again. "You ought to know by now, son, that girls these days are as rugged as we are. And then some."

"I don't care, the place isn't— Oh, what the hell!" What did it matter, anyway, Henry thought sulkily. He hadn't really intended to go out there himself, but he might as well, and let them come, too, if they must. Maybe the girl could cook, and Claude would buy some groceries, and they'd have a few decent meals. He was starving right now.

The cab turned into Claude's street, and Henry sat up and adjusted his tie. Claude gave him a sidelong look.

"You needn't bother to slick up for Diana. I happen to know that she thinks your skull is sharply lacking in interior decoration."

"Does she think the fatty stuffing in yours is more attractive?"

Claude heaved himself out of the cab and left Henry to pay for the fare. As they mounted the steps, Gilling smiled down at them from the door in an almost paternal fashion.

"I have news of Evans. His wife had a note from him. He is away on important, confidential business."

Chapter 11

CLAUDE AND HENRY looked at Gilling in cold silence, and he went on smoothly, "Why didn't you tell me, Mr. Boster, that you had sent Mr. Evans away on important and confidential business?"

"Outside of it having nothing to do with you," Claude snarled, "I did not send him away on business of any sort."

Gilling turned to Henry. "Do you know anything about it?"

Henry said, "No," indifferently, and Claude demanded, "Why don't you get Scrimmer? What has Evans to do with it, anyway? You've no right to be butting into his private affairs."

Gilling stood aside without further words and allowed them to pass into the house. He made no attempt to follow them, and Henry, glancing over his shoulder, saw him slowly walk down the steps and cross the street.

Claude had gone into the living room and was talking excitedly to Diana, and as Henry came in she was saying firmly, "I have shopping to do. After all, I live a lot in the country, and when I come to the city, I want to stay and enjoy it. Why don't you go? You and your precious Henry? Have all the fun you want, and I'll stay here with the bright lights."

She gave Henry a baleful look, but he was leaning against the wall with his hands in his pockets and merely shrugged. It was no concern of his. They could settle it between them.

Claude looked at him and quivered all over with fury. He yelled, "Get busy, you damned tailor's dummy, and persuade her to come, or you're fired!"

Henry raised his eyebrows. "You should always use the direct approach. It's much simpler in the end." He turned to Diana. "There's an escaped convict who has it in for your papa, and he's been flinging bullets around rather recklessly, therefore the old man thinks we'd all be safer out in the country."

Diana looked quickly from one to the other of them, and Claude howled, "Wad'ya mean by blurting it out like that! I told you I didn't want her frightened!"

Henry removed himself from the wall and went to the window, where he took an appraising look at the sky. He said, "Either you're coming with me, or not. Make up your minds. It's going to snow, and I want to get out there before the roads get bad."

It took Diana a certain amount of time to make up her mind and an even longer time to pack and get ready, once she had decided to go. Henry made frequent trips to the front door, calling a firm good-bye over his shoulder, but was bullied or persuaded back each time by Claude.

When the girl was ready at last, Claude ordered his car to be sent around from the garage. He loaded her luggage and his own into it, put her carefully into the back seat with a rug over her knees, and climbed in beside her. He called to Henry, "Come on, get in and drive us out to your blasted shack, and hurry, because it's getting late."

Henry got in, and asked between gritted teeth, "What about *my* packing? You two have enough stuff to last you for a month, and I suppose you expect me to get along with what I stand up in."

"Don't try to hand me that!" Claude shouted. "I've been out there, and I know you keep a set of essentials, including a bunch of old clothes. You don't need anything, and you know it."

This was all too true, but Henry was in a mood to create difficulties. He slumped down behind the wheel and folded his arms.

"O.K.," Claude said bitterly. "You make a nice target for Pitty, anyway."

Henry was shaken to the point of saying sulkily, "Give me the keys and the girl and I'll get started."

Claude threw the keys over into the front seat, and Henry fitted them into the lock. "I said the girl too."

"What the devil are you talking about?" Claude howled. "For God's sake, get going, before you get a bullet bounced off your concrete skull."

"I want company," Henry said stubbornly. "Why should I sit up here all alone, no one to talk to, nothing to do? You can amuse yourself back there with memories of your long-lost youth, but I'm only a boy, and I need young companions." He leaned his head against the back of the seat and began to whistle.

There was a short silence, and then Diana said urgently, "Papa! Stop it! Your blood pressure! For heaven's sake, what does it matter? Here, take the rug."

She scrambled over into the front seat, settled herself, and gave Henry a chilly eye. "Will you start now?"

"Of course. Certainly."

As he pulled the car away from the curb, he saw Gilling on the sidewalk, gazing after them with his usual owl-like stare. Henry could not resist making a face at him and then had to jam the brake on to avoid hitting a car he had not seen.

Diana said, "Heaven preserve us! Are you that kind of driver?"

"Yes."

It was a two-hour drive, and they did the greater part of it in silence. The heater was out of order, and as time went on they all became cold and cross. Henry wished fervently that he had never mentioned his house and thought longingly of the warm hotel room he had abandoned. Diana called herself a fool half-a-dozen times, and Claude wondered out loud why any fool would own a house in this bleak, God-forsaken part of the country.

They came at last to a small village, and Henry pulled up in front of the grocery store with a sigh of relief.

"This is the last outpost of civilization before we reach my house." He glanced at Diana and added, "You'd better come in and market for whatever it is you'll want to cook."

She looked at him, and then burst into clear, happy laughter. "This really makes me feel a bit better. My mother always wanted me to be a pianist, so she never would let me spoil my hands in the kitchen. I can't even make toast. It always goes black."

"That's fine," Henry said bitterly. "I can't cook myself."

Claude started lumbering out of the back seat and swearing at the same time. "It's come to a pretty pass when a man of my age and standing has to cook for three people in order to eat. But it's not going on for long, by God. I'm going to damned well teach you both, and you're going to pay attention, or live on black toast. I wish I'd got on the boat with Fred."

They all went into the grocery, and while Diana and Henry wandered around buying whatever happened to please them, Claude arranged for the necessary staples and food for several meals with swift and precise executive ability.

When they left the store, loaded and panting, they found it was snowing. Diana dropped her load into the back seat and said petulantly, "I'm cold and I'm hungry. Where can we have dinner?"

"We can have dinner at the house," Henry said, sliding under the wheel. "There are no restaurants around here, and anyway, we'd better get out there before the snow gets deep. I have to start the furnace, too."

"Furnace!" Diana moaned. "The house will be bone cold! Papa, darling, can't we go somewhere and get a decent meal while he gets the furnace started?"

"You cannot," Henry said decisively. "I'm starving, and while I light the furnace, Papa's going to prepare dinner."

"If you ever," said Claude, in a low, quivering voice, "call me 'Papa' again, I shall do the job on you that Scrimmer messed up."

The snow was beginning to fall heavily, and Henry started the windshield wipers and drove carefully out of the village and onto a deserted country road. It was bordered by dark, bare trees, and the only sound was made by their own car. Diana huddled against the door, looking gloomily out at the darkening, snow-blown woods and wincing when the car skidded on the frozen ruts. The road seemed to go on interminably, but at last Henry slowed and turned carefully into a driveway that stretched ahead into a mass of trees and shrubbery. There was no sign of the house until Henry made another turn, which unexpectedly brought them directly in front of it. Diana stared, and gave forth a hollow moan. "It's haunted! It must be!"

"Certainly it's haunted," Henry said composedly. "My aunt always declared she'd never leave it, dead or alive. She's dead now, but since she was a woman of her word, I assume she still lives here. I thought of putting you in her bedroom—be company for you both."

"Shut up, you damned fool! Trying to scare a delicate girl!" Claude yelled. "Help me in with this stuff, and then you can put the car in the garage."

"Barn," said Henry. "And it was never built to house a gadget like this car of yours, either."

Claude threw a parcel into his arms, but he let it slide through and down onto the snow.

"Don't be in such a hurry," he said coldly. "I have to look for the keys—find out whether I brought them with me or not."

"Oh, please!" Diana, hugging herself with her arms, stamped feebly on the ground. "Can't you hurry? I'm simply frozen."

"It's warmer out here than it is in there," Henry observed, making a great deal of noise with a jingling key ring.

"Come on, come on, come on," Claude growled.

"All right. I have it. It's the key for the side door, where the electric switch is. You wait here, and I'll come through and open the front door for you."

He disappeared into the falling snow, and Diana raised her head to look at the house. It was almost dark by now, and the snow was thick, but after a certain amount of peering she turned to Claude and cried shrilly, "Papa, did you know? The whole house is painted black!"

Chapter 12

HENRY OPENED the front door as Diana spoke and said, "Come on in. My aunt had this place painted black because she figured that way she'd never have to do it again."

"She was cracked in the head," Claude said briefly, ushering Diana in with a hand on her arm.

Henry closed the door after them. "She was not cracked in the head. The members of my family have always been quite normal mentally."

"I suppose you really believe that." Claude dropped a suitcase onto the floor and shook snow from his hat. "Matter of fact, the entire gang was about one step ahead of the wagon."

"Will you two shut up," Diana wailed, "and get some heat up here before I freeze solid?"

"Oh, well"—Henry took her arm—"I am not in the mood for gallantry, but blood will tell. Come on." He led her from the square entrance hall down a narrow passage that passed a narrow flight of stairs and turned into a room at the left. He switched on the lights, and she saw that the room was huge and furnished in a rather jumbled fashion as a dining room. At the far end a few easy chairs were grouped around the fireplace and a small electric heater stood in the fireplace itself. Henry turned the switch, and almost at once the little heater began to glow comfortably.

He said, "There. Sit in front of the thing and get warm while I go down and light the blasted furnace." He turned to Claude, who had come in behind them, and added, "Perhaps you could start cooking."

"Perhaps I could," Claude said nastily, "and then, again, perhaps I couldn't. In fact, if I'm the cook, I'll do the cooking when and if I get hungry."

Henry sat down in a chair in front of the heater and stretched his legs to it. "O.K., then I'll light the furnace when and if I get cold."

Claude extended a wet shoe toward the heater and said with cold dignity, "You are behaving like a five-year-old child."

"No five-year-old child is as smart as I am—not even when I was five years old."

"Ahh, for God's sake!" Claude changed feet and held the other one out. "Anyway, it so happens that I am hungry now."

"That's odd," Henry murmured. "I'm beginning to get cold now, too."

"Is there a telephone here?" Diana asked abruptly.

Henry looked at her. "Why?"

"I want to phone that crook who's been trying to shoot us and tell him where we are. He can come here and put us all out of our misery."

"Very amusing," Henry said politely.

He and Claude went to a swinging door which opened into a large butler's pantry and on to the kitchen, where Henry turned on the light. The kitchen was only slightly larger than the pantry, and Claude glanced around without much interest.

"You don't have a broiler," he said irritably. "You said you'd get one when I was out here on that weekend party back when you were trying to impress me. God! Was I bored!"

"So was I," said Henry and started down the steps to the cellar. He went first to the coal bin with his fingers crossed. He couldn't remember how much coal he had left, but he breathed again when he saw that there was enough.

The hot-air furnace was a large, old-fashioned coal-burning affair, and there was a small pot-bellied stove beside it to furnish hot water. Both were filled with cold, dead gray ashes, and Henry sighed and sought a shovel.

Upstairs in the dining room Diana began to feel considerably better as time went on. A faint warmth that did not come from the electric heater began to be noticeable, and there was a decided smell of cooking food from the direction of the butler's pantry. She got up after a while and went to stand over the hot-air register. This was much better. Heat was pouring up in a comforting billow, and she was able to remove her coat. Her skirt belled out around her, and she gave a sigh of content and lit a cigarette. She strayed off the register once or twice to examine the room, but she always returned quickly. It was still very cold away from the direct heat.

Henry appeared suddenly, bearing a large feather duster, and began to flip it around the room. Diana stared at him.

"What on earth do you think you're doing?"

"Dusting."

"Nonsense. You're simply chasing the dust around the room from one object to another."

"One thing about hot-air heat," Henry said, still flipping, "is that it comes up quickly. And as far as this dusting goes, I am not chasing it around the room. The dust all goes into the feathers. My aunt used to say that no modern method could compare with the feather duster."

"The more I hear about her," Diana said tolerantly, "the more I wonder how she managed to stay even one step ahead of the wagon."

Henry sneezed loudly and put the duster away. "There, now the room's clean. We can sit down and have some sherry while we're waiting for dinner."

He went to an immense old sideboard, swung open a door, and began to feel around inside while bottles clattered together warningly.

"Isn't there anything but sherry?" Diana asked.

"Sherry and port and a few other assorted wines. My aunt didn't approve of spirits."

"Well," Diana sighed, "that's one thing the old girl and I have in common. I don't approve of her, and you tell me she's a spirit."

"Ha, ha," Henry said politely.

He brought four glasses and wiped them with a napkin he had taken from a drawer. The napkin became black, but Diana ignored it and merely asked, "Why four glasses?"

"One for Auntie," Henry said, pouring carefully.

Claude came in from the pantry, wiping his hands on the sides of his trousers.

"Here's a glass of sherry for you, Papa," Diana told him, "but don't take Henry's aunt's ghost's glass, because she likes to drink it herself."

Henry nodded. "She may take her time about it, but she does like to drink it herself."

Claude sniffed the sherry, and his eyebrows went up. He sipped, and then observed almost amiably, "Mad as hares, all those Debbons."

He drank the wine, put down the glass, and headed back for the kitchen. "Dinner's almost ready," he called over his shoulder. "In fact, you can come out now."

Henry glanced at Diana. "Someone had better set the table."

Claude paused, with the swinging door held open. "We're eating in the kitchen," he said flatly.

"Oh no," Henry protested. "This room has been properly dusted, and anyway, I don't like—"

"You are eating in the kitchen," Claude said distinctly, "or you are not eating at all."

Henry said, "We are eating in the kitchen."

Diana took her sherry and went to stand over the register again. Henry went into the kitchen and distributed some knives and forks around the table. The stove had made it comfortably warm there, and when they presently sat down to the meal, they were almost cheerful.

Henry discovered at once that Claude was an expert with the skillet. The only drawback was that he expected—and got—praise after nearly every mouthful, but the meal was worth it.

When they had finished, Claude lit a cigar and Diana started a cigarette. Henry, after waiting in silence, and unsuccessfully, brought out a cigarette and said pointedly, "I'd have liked a cigar."

"Nothing like a good cigar after a good meal," Claude agreed composedly. "Not knowing how long we'd be out here, I brought a fair supply with me."

"Of course," Henry said bitterly. "You won't want for anything. You never do. But what about me? I came straight out here just to accommodate you, and I wasn't given time to get anything, not even my book."

"Too bad," Claude murmured, puffing contentedly. "You don't need a book, anyway. Just let me know when you're in a literary mood, and I'll tell you a story."

"You can tell me one right now. All about Scrimmer."

"What d'ya mean? You know I'm not holed in in this blasted, ugly, ghost-ridden old black warehouse because I like the country air."

"Now, Papa," Diana said mildly, "it's really an interesting old place."

Henry gave her a little bow, murmured, "Thank you," and then turned to Claude.

"Scrimmer went into your office and did not come out. I was there all the time, and I know he didn't. You went in there shortly afterward and you saw him because you must have seen him. There are no hiding places in that room. So what's the story?"

Claude began to chew agitatedly on his cigar, and his face reddened. "What about Fred and Miss Robb?" he demanded belligerently. "They were in my office too. Do you think we're all in a conspiracy?"

Henry shook his head. "He could hide in there if he had your cooperation. You probably put him under the desk and shoved your big feet on him. I want to know the story, and I think I have a right to know it, since either he or you is taking potshots at me."

Claude stood up from the table, and Diana came around and put a hand on his arm. "Now, Papa, remember your blood pressure."

"If I had a gun right now," Claude said thickly, "I'd take a potshot

that would do more than graze his blasted, impudent face. I'd kill him—
I'd—"

He was making for the pantry, and Diana followed, still patting his
arm. "But, Papa, he was only asking. I don't see why you get so furious."

Claude stopped with the swinging door half open and turned on her.

"What are you sticking up for him for? Are you getting soft on him?
I warn you here and now that it won't do him any good, because I'll
murder him with my bare hands before I'll see him married to you!"

Diana's only answer was a shrill scream. Claude gave a nervous
leap, and Henry stared with his mouth open. She was looking through
the half-opened door into the dining room, and Claude peered over her
shoulder. "What is it, baby?" he asked in a shaken voice. "I don't see
anything."

"There. In there on the table," she whispered. "Auntie's ghost drank
the sherry."

Chapter 13

HENRY WALKED into the dining room and then directed a stern look
at Claude. He said to Diana, "Why don't you ask your dear papa what
became of the sherry, instead of accusing an innocent ghost?"

"Bah!" Claude said hoarsely. "You drank it yourself."

Diana shook her head. "No, no, I remember noticing it when we
went to dinner, and neither one of you has been out of the kitchen since.
Oh, Papa! There's someone in the house!"

Claude and Henry looked at each other for a moment, and then
Claude took a long breath. "Nonsense! Rubbish! You've made a mistake, baby. Go on, Henry, and wash the dishes. I did the cooking."

Diana said quietly, "I didn't make a mistake."

Henry raised his voice to almost a bellow. "I'm not going to wash
the dishes. Diana ought to do them. She hasn't done anything yet."

"I'm not going to stay in any of these rooms alone," Diana declared
emphatically.

Claude sat down on one of the dining-room chairs and puffed at his
cigar. "Henry will wash the dishes, baby, but you go and help him. He'll

be right there with you, and you won't have to worry. As for the sherry, I remember quite well now that he got up while we were eating and went and drank it."

"Who, me?" Henry demanded, astounded.

Claude scowled at him. "Yes, you."

"I did nothing of the sort."

"You've forgotten it, that's all, but I remember it quite distinctly. That sherry was on your mind, and you automatically went and drank it. After trying to scare Diana with a silly story about your aunt's ghost, you couldn't stand seeing the stuff go to waste."

Henry took in breath for a loud and indignant denial, and then saw that Diana's frightened eyes were on his face. He expelled the breath and turned back into the butler's pantry.

"All right, anything you say, Mr. Boster. Come on, Diana, we'll get these dishes done."

He made her wash, because he said he knew where things belonged and could put them away after he'd dried them. He proceeded to hand her back at least half the dishes she had washed with a stern order to do them better, but he was obliged to stop this abruptly when she finally threw one of them on the floor. He observed bitterly that it had been a piece of Limoges.

"I don't care whether it was Royal Turkey," Diana said crossly. "You can just wipe the stuff off on your towel."

Henry wiped the rest of the stuff off on his towel.

When they had finished, they went back into the dining room and discovered that Claude had gone.

"Where is he?" Diana asked fearfully. "I'm afraid. This place scares me. I know you didn't drink that sherry, and I think we ought to search the house. There's someone creeping around in here with us. Maybe Papa is searching the house now. Do you think so?"

Henry walked out into the hall, where the lights had been turned on. He said loudly, "You're behaving like a silly kid. He's looking for a bathroom, that'a all."

"Well, for that matter, so am I. Take me to one."

"Come on." Henry started up the stairs. "There's only one. Up this way."

"You have only one bathroom in a house of this size?"

"You're out in the country," Henry said coldly. "Even one bathroom is a luxury."

There was a light in the hall upstairs, and the bathroom door was closed. Henry gestured toward it. "You see? Now we'll have to wait in line."

"Well, I'm next," Diana said firmly. "I mentioned it first."

"I'll concede that."

Diana looked around her and said wonderingly, "This house is really very peculiar. The stairs are so narrow and the hall downstairs too. Up here the hall is much wider."

Henry nodded. "I thought I'd told you. My aunt put a partition squarely through the center of the house, and the other side is just like this. She made a sort of two-family arrangement out of it, or semidetached. She had to install a bathroom on the other side, and of course there was no butler's pantry over there. The kitchen, which is the other half of our kitchen here, has more modern equipment, too, since it was done more recently."

"How queer!" Diana breathed. "You'd think it would have been impossible."

Henry shrugged. "This house lent itself to such an arrangement. It's a sort of double-breasted place."

"Does anyone live in there?"

Henry shook his head. "Not now. She did have one or two tenants, but it was never easy to rent."

Claude flung open the bathroom door and emerged, and Diana asked, "Are there any towels in there?"

Claude nodded. "There's a closet full of them. Lot of 'em stolen from the best hotels, and there's a hand towel I know for a fact comes from my office. I'm taking it back with me."

"You'll take no towel out of this house," Henry declared heatedly. "The proof that it doesn't come from your office is the fact that it has no holes in it."

Diana went into the huge bathroom and said, "Don't go away. I might have to call for help if I fall into that tub. I wouldn't be able to crawl out again."

She shut the door, and Claude laughed. "She's quite a gal, my baby. Matter of fact, that's the only bathtub I've ever seen that I consider large enough for me." He stepped closer to Henry and lowered his voice. "Did you or did you not drink that sherry?"

"I did not," Henry said emphatically.

Claude rattled the change in the pockets of his trousers and carefully regarded his shoes.

"We'll search the place tomorrow," Henry said presently.

"Why not tonight?"

Henry rumpled his hair fretfully. "Because I'm too tired, and I'm not alert enough to dodge even Scrimmer's lousy aim."

"You're as cracked as all the rest of the Debbons," Claude said peevishly. "How can you possibly sleep when you know he may be prowling around?"

"You think it really is Scrimmer?"

"How do I know who it is?" Claude glanced uneasily over his shoulder. "But I don't want to get shot in my sleep. Besides, there's Diana to think of."

"We can go into my aunt's suite," Henry said. "She has bars and bolts on the doors, and once we're locked in, nobody will be able to get to us."

"All right, but how the hell did he get in in the first place? Didn't you shut the doors after you?"

Henry thought it over. "I believe I left the side door open when I came through to let you in at the front. I suppose someone could have followed me in. Maybe it's just a tramp. But it seems to me more likely that one of us drank that wine and simply forgot about it. Anyway, we'll search the place tomorrow."

"I'll have to phone," Claude said restlessly, "and see whether the police have a line on Scrimmer."

"Not from here. There isn't any phone. You know that."

"Oh, for God's sake!" Claude howled. "That's you Debbons all over. Rotting away in the country without even a phone. How can anyone live without a phone!"

"Never mind the Debbons," Henry said coldly. "You haven't told me yet what you and Scrimmer talked about when you went into your office and found him waiting there for you."

Claude swelled, and his face reddened, but before he could say anything Henry added, "There's no use in losing your temper, because if you don't tell me, I'm going to Gilling about it."

"You can tell Gilling any Goddamn thing you like," Claude hissed, with a glance at the bathroom door.

It opened as he finished speaking, and Diana emerged, obviously shivering. "Why isn't there any heat in there?" she demanded.

"There is," Henry said with quiet dignity, "but it happens to be in the linen closet. That closet was put in long after the furnace, and the only place for it was over the hot-air register. It keeps the towels warm, anyway."

"Stop drooling," Claude muttered, "and show us this blasted suite with all its locks and bars."

The suite consisted of two rooms with a connecting door, and the doors leading to the hall were well fortified with various bolts. The floors and all the furniture had a liberal coating of dust.

Diana, looking around her, said, "Oh, God. Where's that damned feather duster?"

"You may sleep in the bedroom," Henry said formally, "and Mr. Boster and I will use the sitting room, which is equipped with two day beds."

Diana looked at him. "Why?"

"Why not?"

"Why can't you get another room somewhere else?" Claude demanded.

"I mean, why are there two day beds in the sitting room?" Diana asked.

Henry gritted his teeth for a moment, and then relaxed enough to explain, "My aunt's two girlfriends used to be afraid to sleep anywhere else in this house."

"Why were they afraid?" Diana asked simply.

"Will you," Claude asked Henry with ominous patience, "kindly go down and bring up some of the suitcases?"

"I want to go and get my own personal supplies from my room first," Henry explained.

"If you have your own things in another room, why don't you stay there?" Claude demanded. "I'm damned if I want you sleeping in with me. I have an idea that you snore."

"Entirely mutual," Henry said frigidly, "but nothing can be done about it."

"What do you mean, nothing can be done about it? Doesn't your door have a lock on it?"

"No," said Henry.

"Papa," Diana interposed in an exasperated voice, "for heaven's sake get some sheets so that we can make up the beds. I'm simply exhausted." She picked up a scarf from the bureau and started dusting with it.

Henry stared at her, fascinated. He had never in his life been allowed to touch those scarfs, and here was this girl using one of them as a duster. He thought of his aunt and shivered, as though she had reached over and touched him with an icy, accusing finger for allowing such desecration. And then he shivered again because he remembered, suddenly, why his aunt's girlfriends had been so afraid of the house. They had declared that some disembodied spirit always drank their wine if they left it alone for any length of time.

Chapter 14

HENRY SHOOK his head a little and tried to clear his thoughts. He had always known the true explanation of that wine business. His aunt had been a bit too fond of it and didn't like people to know how much she drank. If her friends left full glasses unguarded, she quietly imbibed the wine and said nothing. Only, that didn't explain the sherry tonight. Henry knew that no one had left the kitchen, and yet the glass had been emptied. They ought to search the house, of course, but it would be so difficult. A good many of the rooms were without electric bulbs, and he had no flashlight. There might be one around the house somewhere—probably was—but he did not know where. Well. Henry shrugged. It was a cold, snowy night, and if a tramp had wandered in, let him stay.

Diana, fussing with the beds, asked him crossly, "Why don't you help?"

"What do you want me to do?"

Claude came back from the bathroom where he had been getting sheets.

"Stupid place to have a linen closet," he grumbled. "All these things must be damp after anyone takes a shower."

"Anyone doesn't take a shower," said Henry shortly. "There isn't one. You bathe in the tub."

"You ought to have a life preserver hanging on that tub," Claude observed, dropping the sheets onto the bed. "Someone's going to drown there one of these days."

The bed-making turned out to be decidedly slipshod. Diana knew a little more about it than the other two but was far from expert. Two of the sheets were badly torn and had to be replaced, and then they discovered that they had no blankets or pillows, and had to start a search for them.

"Remind me to kill myself if I ever come out here again," Claude said savagely.

Henry tried to brush an accumulation of dust from the front of his shirt. "People who force themselves on your hospitality are always the most discourteous guests."

Diana said suddenly, "Wait a minute. I know where they'd be. In the bottom drawers of the bureau. Come on, let's look."

She was right as far as the blankets were concerned, but there were no pillows in the drawers and they were unable to find any. Diana and Henry declared that they'd sleep without, but Claude bellowed so vociferously that Henry eventually ran downstairs and got him a cushion from the couch in the dining room. Claude took it without gratitude and complained that it was too hard.

"So's your head," Henry said in exasperation.

"Oh, go to your room, both of you," Diana groaned. "Only leave the door open between, and make sure that your hall door is locked."

Claude pushed Henry into the sitting room and said good night to Diana over his shoulder. They undressed in silence and climbed into the two day beds. One was a studio couch and the other a low cot. Claude automatically took the studio couch, and then took a good fifteen minutes to complain about the mattress and other uncomfortable features.

Henry, sitting straight up because he had no pillow to lean back on, was smoking a cigarette. "If you hadn't indulged your soft body for so many years, you wouldn't be suffering now. Anyway, forget it. I want to know what connection you have with Pitty Scrimmer."

Claude gave tongue to some really colorful swearing, and Henry calmly waited for a break, when he said firmly, "I know you saw Scrimmer, and that you tried to pretend you hadn't. Why?"

Claude swore on, and eventually used an expression that was new to Henry, but he sternly put aside an irrelevant desire to ask what it meant and where Claude had picked it up. Instead, he said, "I'm going to confer with Gilling and I'll have to tell him about your having seen Scrimmer."

"You can tell him until your tongue hangs out," Claude said explosively, "and I'll go on denying it just as long."

"It won't do you any good to deny it. The evidence is irrefutable."

"Big words like that," said Claude, punching his sofa cushion, "don't match your silly face."

"No," said Henry, "but the words you were using a minute ago—and you'll forgive me for saying so—match your face very well. But to come back to the point. I want to know what's going on, the whole story. I have been shot at twice."

"Pity he missed you."

"If you say so. But I still want to know what connection you and Scrimmer—"

"Will you," said Claude, "shut your smug lawyer's face? I want to go to sleep."

"No. I'll keep this up all night if I have to. I want an answer."

Claude closed his eyes and turned over.

"I suppose you and Scrimmer had some sort of a deal on, and Scrimmer came back to get his share. My guess is that you twisted him some way." Henry put out his cigarette in a china hair receiver that he had removed from the bureau. "I wonder where he went? I can see now how you were able to swing that deal last summer, what with all Scrimmer's crooked money in your pocket."

Claude, having exhausted his profanity, merely said, "I am going to do something about having you mad Debbons put on the inside where you belong. Civic duty."

Diana called from the other room, "Will you two please shut up and let me sleep?"

Henry raised his voice a little. "Perhaps she knows about it. I think I'll go in and ask her. Tell her what I know and find out what she knows."

Claude sat up and hissed in an agonized whisper, "Hush, hush, for God's sake! I'll tell you if you'll only be quiet."

"Good. But don't try to pull a phony, because I'll know it at once."

"Stop talking," Claude hissed venomously, "and listen if you want to hear it. I did meet Scrimmer in my office yesterday morning, and it bowled me right over. I didn't want anyone to know he'd come straight to me, naturally. I knew he was out for revenge. He had a gun in his hand and I had to talk fast. I told him if he shot me he couldn't get away, and he'd burn for it, but if he behaved himself, I'd let him go. I figured the police would pick him up pretty quickly anyway, but I wanted Diana protected in the meantime, and that's why I called you into this."

Henry said, "Oh," and fell silent. He didn't believe Claude, but he was tired, and it seemed useless to prod further. At least Claude had admitted seeing Scrimmer, and that was something. Claude was quiet now, and Henry wondered if he'd gone to sleep. Probably not. He didn't feel much like sleeping himself. There was too much to think about. He stretched out on the cot, pulled the blankets up around his neck, and prepared to think the thing out thoroughly and logically.

He awoke at six to a reluctant dawn and the sound of snow tapping busily against the window. He turned over, prepared once more to think the whole thing out, and was asleep again immediately. Claude woke him some time later by shaking his shoulder and saying aggrievedly, "This blasted house is as cold as the North Pole."

Henry groaned and tried to crawl under the blankets, but Claude flung them off. "I tell you you'll have to do something. I've got saliva frozen onto my teeth."

Henry groaned again and crawled out. He crept, shivering, into his clothes, because he knew from experience not to try to work in the cellar wearing only a robe and slippers.

He went through Diana's room and downstairs, yawning and rubbing his cold hands together. In the cellar he found that his two carefully banked fires in the furnace and the pot-bellied stove were still alight, and he grunted with satisfaction. He had learned to be careful about banking those fires at night, since a careless job meant raking out cold ashes and starting all over again in the morning. He opened up all the drafts and mounted the stairs with the comforting thought that there would soon be heat and hot water.

Claude was preparing breakfast in the kitchen, and he turned around from a frying pan with a fresh grievance.

"You left my car out and it's covered with snow. Go and get it into the barn."

Henry considered a curt refusal and then thought better of it, because he was hungry and didn't want the breakfast spoiled.

He had a considerable amount of trouble with the car. It was necessary to wipe a heaped accumulation of snow off the windshield, to put chains on the rear wheels, and, finally, to shovel a rough runway to the door of the barn. He got it in at last, and left it, dripping and seeming to sneer at him, while he closed the door on it.

He was on the vacant side of the house, and as he plodded through the heavy snow he thought for a moment that he saw a light in one of the windows, but when he looked more closely, it was quite blank. His eyes roamed over the black bulk of the house with the snow whirling coldly around it, and he muttered, "Hideous old wreck." It was no wonder that you thought of ghosts and hauntings when you looked at it, but on the other hand, it had been odd about the sherry last night. Oh, well, if there was anyone in the house with them, outside of Auntie, they'd soon find it out. Whoever it was would have to eat, and they'd watch their own supplies. Better search the place anyway this morning. That was a job, when you came to think of it. Rooms, and in some cases even closets, opening into one another on the second and third floors.

He plowed around to the porch and noticed that his own footprints from the front door were already nearly obliterated by the heavily falling snow.

In the kitchen Diana and Claude were sitting at the table. Claude seemed unusually quiet, but Diana told Henry that his breakfast was in the oven, and he automatically turned to the old coal range that his aunt had used for so many years. He had put his hand on its chilly bulge before he remembered to turn to the electric stove.

The breakfast was as good as the dinner had been, and Henry became genial enough to offer a compliment, but Claude merely said, "Ahh, shut up," rather absently.

Diana smiled at Henry and said amiably, "It's a pity you put the car away. I'm going back to town today. I think it was silly to come out here in the first place."

"You won't go by car," Henry told her. "You couldn't get it two yards beyond the barn right now, and the snow is still coming down. They don't plow this road, either."

"What about a train?"

"Station's five miles from here."

"Oh, for heavens' sake!" Diana looked appealingly at Claude. "There must be *some* way to get out of here." Claude shook his head rather helplessly, and Henry offered, "There's a bus about a mile away, but when the weather gets bad, they usually just quit. It saves wear and tear on the busses and the drivers."

Diana made an exasperated sound and flounced off into the dining room, and Henry turned to Claude.

"By the way, was there any food missing from the icebox this morning?"

Claude's face seemed to crumple, and little drops of moisture sprang out on his forehead. He looked down at his shaking hands and mumbled, "Oh, God! I'm frightened!"

Chapter 15

HENRY WAS surprised and showed it. He had never seen Claude give way to weakness like this before. After a moment he said, "So there was some food missing?"

Claude took out a cigar and lit it. His hands were shaking slightly, but when he spoke, his voice had the usual aggressive quality. "Yes, some of the stuff was gone."

Henry nodded. "We'd better start a search now, then. I suppose some tramp came in after us last night."

"Yes, yes, of course. A tramp." Claude stood up. "We'll find him and throw him out."

He left the kitchen, followed by Henry, and in the dining room they found Diana standing by one of the windows, staring out into the falling snow.

Claude stopped and eyed her uneasily, and Henry suggested, "We'd better take her with us."

"It might be dangerous."

"It might be dangerous to leave her here."

Diana turned from the window and frowned at them. "Why don't you talk *to* me instead of *about* me? You'd think I was a child. What danger are you rushing into now with your swords bared?"

"We're going to search the house," Henry said easily, "and we think you'd better come with us. It's possible that a tramp might have sneaked in after us last night."

"Oh." She looked them over coldly.. "I don't see why on earth we came out here in the first place. The whole thing is absurd."

Henry shrugged. "Anything you say. But you'd better come with us now."

"Please, baby," Claude wheedled. "It won't take long."

She followed them as they headed for the stairs and impatiently brushed cigar ash from Claude's sleeve. "What difference does it make how long it takes? What have I to do until lunchtime except bite my nails and look at the snow? I might as well come along and watch you two play cops and robbers." But she felt a little contrite as she followed them up the stairs. After all, this was supposed to be a dangerous mission, and she shouldn't make fun of them.

The dangerous mission took them all the way up to the attic, which was on the third floor. They stationed Diana at the head of the stairs, and Henry said, "Scream like hell if a strange man appears."

"I don't like it," Claude muttered.

"You start at the back, and I'll start at the front," Henry instructed him firmly. "There are only three rooms here, but they open into each other, so we'll meet in the middle of the middle room. See?"

Claude, chewing nervously on his cigar, said, "Mad as hares, all of you," but started off obediently.

It did not take them long to meet in the middle of the middle room, but when they went back into the hall, Diana was no longer standing at the head of the stairs.

Claude let out a terrified bellow. "Baby! Where are you?"

She answered at once, in a muffled voice that came from the front room. "For heavens' sake, Papa, I'm here. I'm all right."

She emerged from a shallow closet as they came in, "I've already looked in there. No one in it," said Henry.

"I know, but there's a door here in the back wall of the closet. Doesn't it lead into the other side of the house?"

"Yes, but it should be locked."

"It is locked, but I don't think from this side. I think it's bolted on the other side."

"No, it isn't." Henry tried to get into the closet to have a look, but Claude pushed in ahead of him. "The door is locked on this side. I know because my aunt lost the key for it and was very upset. She liked to be able to sneak in and snoop on her tenants whenever she felt like it."

"Yale lock," Claude muttered. "It's locked, all right, and there's no key here." He came out dusting his hands. "Maybe you could find the key and we can get in the other side this way."

"We'll finish searching this side first," Henry decided. "She lost all the keys to that side, and I had to get in through a window after she died to look it over. I had some new keys made for the front and back doors."

"It's funny for a person to lose all the keys to a place," Diana murmured.

Claude grunted. "Nothing funny about it when you remember that she was as mad as a hare."

They went down to the second floor, where there were three good-sized rooms and a little sewing room that appeared to have been made out of part of the hall. It had to be searched, since it was jammed with odd bits of furniture, and Claude began a steady swearing under his breath, which grew louder as he blundered through large closets filled with boxes and hung with dusty old clothes.

"Why the damn don't you give your aunt's blasted old rags to the Salvation Army?" he demanded hotly. "Not that they'd want them."

"I had explicit instructions from my aunt before she died that her things were to be left intact. She said she'd be back from time to time and might want to wear them occasionally."

Diana gave a little gasp, and Claude said hastily, "Don't pay any attention to him, baby. He's only a mad Debbon."

They went down to the ground floor, and Henry led the way into a large room at the front. "This is the sitting room and library."

Claude looked around at the clutter of chairs and built-in bookcases. "It's a good thing you told us. We might have mistaken it for the billiard room."

"Then I suppose the parlor or drawing room is at the front on the other side," Diana said, looking about her.

Henry nodded. "The drawing room was almost a young ballroom, and there was a small den behind it which Auntie turned into a butler's pantry, since it opened into the kitchen. She put a partition through the drawing room and made a dining room and living room out of it."

"It was a shame," Diana murmured, "to ruin a lovely old place like this by cutting it up the way she did."

"Quite mad," Claude muttered.

Henry straightened up after looking behind a divan. "So it's a lovely old place now. You had some other names for it awhile ago."

"It *is* a lovely old place. It's just that she sat and thought out one of the best ways to spoil it."

"Quiet," Henry said, "she might hear you."

"We have to search the cellar yet," Claude interposed impatiently. "If you can stop sticking straws in your hair long enough to attend to it."

Henry deliberately made an idiot's face and said, "I'm scared of the cellar. Let's just lock the cellar door instead."

Diana grinned at him. "Feeling good this morning, aren't you?"

They went into the dining room, and Claude started his search by looking under the table. Henry looked under the sofa and observed, "It looks very much as though we were going to be snowed in here. It's coming down more heavily than ever."

Claude shuddered and then roared furiously, "Nonsense! Rubbish! Those clucks must have found Scrimmer by now. We'll go out later and phone."

Henry laughed at him. "You go out and phone. You can leave me here. I've been caught in this place in a snowstorm before, and I've learned that you just stay here until it's over."

Claude mopped his forehead and cursed the snow, and Diana said impatiently, "Come on, will you, and let's finish this search."

They went through the butler's pantry to the kitchen, looked through two closets, and then proceeded on to the dark lobby at the top of the cellar stairs.

"Where's the light?" Claude demanded.

Henry switched it on, but it was only a dim bulb at the foot of the stairs.

"Baby," Claude said uneasily, "you stay up here."

"No, I want to see the cellar too."

She followed them down and then stood looking about her almost in awe. The cellar had not been divided and was a vast, shadowy expanse of stone, concrete, and dust. There were windows on all sides, but the snow had banked up over them and blotted out the light, and the one feeble electric bulb only accentuated the dark corners.

"Your aunt provided the heat for her tenants?" Diana asked.

Henry nodded. "Heat and hot water. It was expensive, but she wouldn't leave the house, and she didn't really have the money to keep it up. She was about broke when she died."

Diana stood under the light while the other two searched. It became obvious to her that neither one of them trusted the other, so that in her opinion the cellar was searched twice. They did it thoroughly, though, and after a while she got impatient.

"Come on, you two, it's cold down here, and there's no one hiding anywhere. Let's go up to the kitchen and have some coffee."

Neither answered her, and they continued to root around in dark corners. She waited for a while, and then went up to the kitchen and put the remains of the breakfast coffee on to heat. She cleared the dirty dishes off the table and piled them in the sink, and then brought out a sugared coffee ring that had caught her fancy in the grocery the night before. She put clean cups around, turned the light off under the coffee, and went to the head of the cellar stairs, where she called down impatiently.

Claude and Henry came tramping up, their heads and clothes draped with cobwebs and dust.

"Dirtiest cellar I've ever set foot in," Claude said, slapping at his trouser legs.

"You haven't set foot in many then. I suppose you always let the other guy do the cellar work, while you—"

"Shut up!" Diana said firmly. "Both of you. I'm sick and tired of all the bickering. It looks as though we were going to be stuck here for a while, so we might as well make the best of it. You can be polite to each other, at least in front of me. When you're alone, you can cut each other's throats for all I care."

"Why, baby—" Claude began, in an injured voice.

She kissed the top of his head. "I didn't mean you, Papa. If he hurts you, I'll kill him. I meant you could cut his throat."

"Go on," Henry said, stirring his coffee. "Pat each other on the back and leave me out in the cold. It doesn't matter if I feel lonely and unwanted."

Diana hacked at the coffee ring and said composedly, "Don't be silly. You have your aunt."

Henry swallowed the too-hot coffee and felt it burning all the way down. He looked at Diana reproachfully, with watering eyes, and Claude let out a roar of laughter. "Those mad Debbons never did need human companionship. Give 'em a Ouija board, they think they're at a cocktail party."

Diana laughed, and Henry said, "I'm beginning to think that Fred is my favorite Boster after all."

Claude draped his face in a cold sneer. "I'll tell Fred that the next time I see him. It'll point up his whole life."

Diana stood up. "Wait a minute. Freeze this fight until I come back. I have to go upstairs and get cigarettes."

She went off and was halfway up the stairs before she realized that someone she could not see was walking quietly up beside her.

Chapter 16

DIANA FROZE halfway up the stairs, and for a moment she stopped breathing. The ghostly footsteps continued until they seemed to reach the top, when they died away into silence. She stood hanging on to the banister, staring at the empty hall above her, until fear drove her stumbling down the stairs and back to the kitchen.

At sight of her Claude jumped to his feet and cried urgently, "What is it, baby? What happened? What's the matter?"

Diana looked from one to the other of them with scared eyes, and whispered, "The ghost."

Henry raised his head from the depleted coffee ring, which was still occupying him, and asked, "Are you referring to my aunt?"

"Tell Papa, baby," Claude wheedled agitatedly. "What was it that frightened you?"

"I was walking up the stairs, and it—it walked up with me. Only I couldn't see it."

"You mean 'she,'" Henry said, "not 'it.'"

Claude glared at him and then mopped his damp brow.

"Come and show us, baby, and explain just what happened."

Henry abandoned the coffee ring and got up. "Yes, you'd better show us just where she was. Chances are, she's all upset because I brought you two out here. I knew she wouldn't like it."

Claude glared again and then patted Diana's shoulder. "Don't listen to him, baby. He's just trying to prove that the Debbons are still mad even after you bury them."

They went out into the hall, and Diana looked fearfully up the stairway. "I was about halfway up when I heard footsteps walking up beside me. I tell you I *heard* them."

Claude shook his head. "You imagined it, baby. You're a little nervous. And no wonder, the way this clown has been carrying on, trying to scare you."

"If Diana says she heard footsteps," the clown said gravely, "then she heard them. She's not the nervous type."

Diana turned on him. "Maybe I'm not, but Papa's right. You're enough to make anyone nervous, and if you mention your demented aunt again, I'll break one of her hideous ornaments over your head."

"You scare me right into being logical," Henry said, squinting up the stairs, "so I'll admit that it might have been someone else who drank the wine and pilfered the food."

Diana widened her eyes. "Someone stole food? Why didn't you tell me?"

"Your papa is determined that you shall lead a sheltered life."

"I'm not at all sure about the food," Claude said soothingly. "I don't count food, and this ape eats so much, it's impossible to tell."

Henry hit the wall with the flat of his hand and squinted up the stairs again. He said to Claude, "She's a big girl now and ready for the facts of life, so stop hedging. The food was gone, and we know that someone is in the house with us, someone besides Auntie, I mean, and he seems to have got through to the other side."

"How could he get through? Claude demanded. "You say it's all locked up."

"Yes, but he's in there, just the same. As you know, the stairs are partitioned through the middle, but it was a cheap job, and you can hear through it without any trouble. On this side the stairs are carpeted, so that the fellow couldn't hear Diana going up, but on the other side there is no carpet, and she heard him quite clearly. It just so happened that they started up the stairs at the same time."

Claude mopped his brow again, and Henry said thoughtfully, "I'm going up to the attic to see if he's using that door in the closet."

Diana followed him, and Claude trailed them, silent and perspiring.

The door in the attic closet proved to be as tightly locked and rusty as before, and Henry turned away from it with a shrug. "I'll get my keys, and we'll go in there through the front door."

Claude, pounding down the attic stairs more quickly than he had gone up, said loudly, "Not me."

"Then you can let me have your gun while I do it."

"What gun?" Claude demanded belligerently.

Henry turned on him impatiently. "Oh, stop wasting time."

"Even if I had a gun, I wouldn't lend it to you."

"Don't be difficult, Papa," Diana said. "He has to protect himself."

"I was merely being courteous," Henry said carelessly. "He's already loaned it to me. The transfer was made last night while he was sleeping."

"You give that gun back to me!" Claude roared furiously.

Henry laughed. "I knew damned well you had one. Come on— give."

Claude felt inside his coat and muttered, "I won't give it to you. I'll go in there with you."

Henry nodded. He linked arms with Diana as they started down to the ground floor and said, "Now listen, you wait here while we go in there, and if we don't show up in twenty minutes, you'd better go for help. You'll have to tramp through the snow, and the nearest place is about half a mile away. You go straight out to the road, turn right, and keep walking until you hit it."

She said, "Oh, God! Why did we come to this horrible place?"

Claude, descending behind them, yelled, "Don't get so chummy with my daughter, or I'll break your blasted arm."

"Sure," said Henry, "then you'll have to take care of the furnace and the pot-bellied stove as well as the cooking. Also the dishwashing, because your daughter is not much good at it."

"Oh, for, God's sake, don't talk so much. Get the damned blasted keys and let's have the thing over with."

"I think they're in my coat pocket." Henry went to the ugly hat rack, shrugged into his overcoat, and felt around in the pocket. "Yes, here they are. Put on your overcoat, Mr. Boster, sir, there's a shutoff in the furnace, and most of that part of the house will be cold."

Diana watched Claude assume his coat and said petulantly, "I don't like staying here alone. I'm afraid."

"Put on your coat and hat, baby," Claude suggested, "and wait out in front."

She glanced out of the window and shivered. "I can't do that, Papa. I'd be cold and my feet would get wet. I'll wait here, but please hurry."

She followed them out onto the wide old porch, keeping close to the wall of the house to avoid the drifting snow. The two front doors were set side by side, and from a short distance away looked like one wide door, and Henry explained that his aunt had had them made to give that impression. Diana watched while he inserted the key and then retreated inside again because she was getting cold. She remained in the hall, close by the door, so that she could run out quickly if anything happened, and wondered, uneasily, why it was that some houses were ghostly and frightening for no particular reason.

In the other side, Henry had been firm about making Claude go first.

"You have the gun," he pointed out. "If you hand it over to me, I'll lead the way, but not otherwise."

Claude muttered, "You're a weak-kneed sissy," but his voice had lost all its belligerence, and Henry glanced at him curiously. His face had sagged, his hands were shaking, and his forehead was beaded with moisture.

He's frightened again, Henry thought, or perhaps he'd been frightened all the time and had been able to cover it up by yelling and snorting. He'd got into something up to his neck, and it was proving too much for him.

Henry reached over and took the gun out of his hand, and instead of the usual infuriated roar, there was only a weak spluttering by way of protest. He drew back and followed Henry almost meekly as they both mounted the stairs.

Henry went all the way to the attic, and Claude lost ground and began to puff badly. He protested, "Can't we look around here first?" but Henry said, "Nope, we'll start at the top and work down."

He made no attempt to be quiet, and his footsteps echoed loudly on the uncarpeted stairs. Claude, panting along behind him, tried to go on tiptoe. He was bitterly regretting the fact that he had given up his gun and was wondering with impotent anger how he had come to do it.

The attic was completely unfurnished, and it took them very little time to discover that there was no one there. They descended to the second floor, which consisted of three sparsely furnished rooms in which the thick dust seemed to be undisturbed, and Henry shook his head. "Don't see how anyone could have been hiding out up here. He'd have to have kicked the dust around a bit."

In the living room, on the ground floor, Henry was conscious of a faint sense of shame. He remembered that the last tenants had wanted to rent the place furnished, and his aunt had picked out a few of her oldest and shabbiest sticks of furniture and set them at intervals around the walls.

The dust was thick here, too, and smooth, as it was in the dining room and the converted butler's pantry. Henry, with his hand on the swinging door that led into the kitchen, cocked an eyebrow at Claude over his shoulder and said, "Come on, this is the last stop."

They went through the door and entered into warmth, and Henry swung up the gun. He said to the man who sat in a chair with his back to them, "Don't move, or I'll shoot," and felt like his small nephew playing cowboys and Indians. He edged around until he was facing the quiet figure in the chair and then lowered the gun.

Claude, standing motionless just inside the door, whispered hoarsely, "What is it?"

Henry glanced up at him and drew a long breath. "Looks as though your troubles are over. It's Scrimmer. And he's dead."

Chapter 17

CLAUDE'S SAGGING face had gone gray, and he began to sway a little on his feet. Henry thought he was going to faint, and he hastened over and caught his arm, but the gesture seemed to pull Claude together. He shook off the steadying hand irritably and muttered, "I don't believe you. You don't know what Scrimmer looks like."

Henry shrugged, and after a moment Claude moved around in front of the still figure. He looked for a while and then closed his eyes, and Henry caught at his arm again.

"Quick!" Claude whispered. "We must get him to a doctor. Do something—"

Henry looked at the dead face with its blank, half-opened eyes and sagging jaw, and said sharply, "Talk sense, can't you? You mean we'd better get him to an undertaker quickly. This room is too warm."

Claude sank onto a chair and passed his handkerchief over his shaking lips, and Henry looked at him curiously. He was badly jolted. No doubt about that. He shrugged again and began to look around the room. The warmth, he knew, was partly owing to the fact that the furnace was almost directly below and partly to a defect in the shutoff, but he discovered that there had been a fire in the coal range. It was out now, but the ashes were still warm. Henry wondered how the man had managed to get coal, since there was no entrance to the cellar from this side of the house. The most puzzling thing, of course, was how he came to be here in the house at all, puzzling because there was only one preposterous explanation. Claude had sent him out here to hide because he knew the place was isolated and unoccupied. Claude had been trying desperately to hide and protect the man. Henry was suddenly furiously angry.

But Claude had had time to think, and he was ready. As Henry turned on him, he said in a loud, shaking voice, "It was Evans. It must have been Evans who brought him out here. They had some sort of a deal together."

Henry, somewhat taken aback, considered it and was obliged to admit to himself that Evans had certainly gone off somewhere. He swallowed his anger for the time being and continued his investigation of the kitchen. There was some evidence that there had been food in the refrigerator, but nothing edible was left.

Claude stirred and said, "For God's sake, let's get out of here."

Henry felt the same way, but he glanced at the body and said hesitantly, "We'd better get him into a colder room."

"Oh, my God!"

"Come on," Henry said impatiently. "We can lift the whole chair. I can't do it alone."

The chair and its gruesome burden proved to be too heavy even for both of them, but they found that they could move it by dragging it along the floor. As they scraped it over the sill into the butler's pantry, the head fell forward and the hat rolled off onto the floor. Claude shuddered but kept doggedly at the task, and at last they deposited the chair in the cold dining room. Henry went back for the hat and replaced it on the sagging head, and Claude shuddered again.

"The wound's at the side of the head here, toward the back," Henry said flatly. "Bullet hole."

Claude turned his eyes away. "We shouldn't have moved him. The police won't like it."

"You don't seem to realize," Henry explained, "that this storm is getting worse. We're not going to be able to get out for a while, and the cooler he is, the better he'll keep."

"You told Diana there was a farmhouse—"

Henry nodded and started for the front door, with Claude trailing him.

"Then why can't we get down there and telephone?"

Henry snorted. "The people who live on that farm don't know yet that the telephone has been invented. They hitch up a horse and jump into a wagon when an emergency occurs, and I'm not going to plow down there and get them and the horse to risk their lives in this storm just for Scrimmer. He's no longer in any hurry."

"My car has good chains—" Claude began uneasily.

"So it has," Henry agreed, "as who should know better than I who had to put them on this morning. You couldn't even get that car out of the barn by now."

Into the silence that followed there came the loud stamping of feet on the front porch. Claude and Henry exchanged a closed, blank look, and then turned together and made for the front door. Henry put a hand on the knob, pulled, and looked out of the crack, while Claude peered over his shoulder. For a moment nothing happened, and then Henry's arm went limp, and he allowed the door to swing wide. He said hollowly, "Ted."

Ted gave him a furious glare and moved toward the door, shedding snow.

"It'll be 'Doctor' to you from now on, you sharp-practice little two-bit lawyer. What do you think my name is down at Memorial Hospital now, except mud? I'll have to go out to the salt mines and hang up a shingle outside a wooden shack, and all because I try to do a favor for a so-called friend."

Claude pushed past Henry out onto the porch and regarded Ted sourly. "Stop yelling your head off. You can come out here to this blasted, lousy house and open up a high-class nut emporium. The atmosphere's right, and Henry can be your first patient, although I doubt whether he's curable."

He made for the other door, and Ted looked after him, suddenly quiet. It was obvious to Henry that the outrageous suggestion was being taken with a certain amount of seriousness, and he had opened his mouth to make a bitter remark when the door was pulled back and Diana's head appeared around it.

"Who's he?" she asked, raising her eyebrows.

Claude patted her cheek as they all trooped into the hall, and Henry murmured, "Just another boarder. We of the noblesse never refuse sanctuary to the meanest of supplicants."

Ted shook himself, and snow drifted, sparkling, to the carpet. He asked abruptly, "Are they here?"

"They?"

"Those two infernal women."

Claude turned away and said, "Come on, baby, let's go to the dining room where it's warmer." He urged her on ahead of him, and Henry followed rooting in his pocket for a cigarette.

Ted hung his coat on the hall rack, removed his rubbers and shoes, stood them near the hot-air register, and padded into the dining room in his socks.

"I asked you—"

"We are not," Henry said repressively, "interested in your women. Why is it that you have to drag a woman with you wherever you go, and sometimes two? Your mind ought to be on your pills."

"These," Ted interrupted coldly, "are not my women. I have never seen them before this morning, and already I find myself disliking them thoroughly. It's all your fault, anyway," he added with sudden anger. "I had to make some sort of gesture of finding you, with your appendix in that state, not that I care whether it blows up and scatters you in a thousand pieces. Anyway, I went to your office this morning, early, and those two women were there. The younger one said that her boss was with you, wherever you were, and the older one said her husband was with the boss, wherever he was. I was silly enough to offer to drive them out here, having no idea that the snow was as bad as it is. I tried to make the driveway, but I went off somewhere, because all of a sudden the car was lying on its side on that stupid, asinine lily pond you have down near the road—my brand-new job on which I still owe everything but the down payment."

"Good heavens!" Diana exclaimed. "Were you hurt? Or the—the ladies?"

Ted turned to her, and his face fell into lines of gracious beauty. "No, dear, only my feelings. We all scrambled out, the ladies yelling like banshees, and they ran off. I stayed to make the car as comfortable as possible, and then came along here."

"You will not," said Claude distinctly, "call my daughter 'dear' ever again."

Ted raised an eyebrow. "I don't work for you, chubby."

"Which way did the women go?" Henry asked.

"Toward the house, here. Where else?"

Henry sighed. "We'll have to find them. I don't know why they didn't come in, but they'll freeze if they stay out there."

"I'm freezing in here," Ted observed, wriggling the toes inside his socks.

"I'll go. You can stay here and thaw out."

Diana stood up. "I'm going with you."

Claude stretched an arm toward her and said, "No, baby, please."

"Now, Papa, don't worry so. I need the air, and it's only snow."

"Snow and him."

Ted laughed cheerfully, and Diana followed Henry out into the hall. She remembered that her coat was upstairs, so she put on Claude's, which was hanging on one of the ugly brass hooks.

"You'd better put a scarf over your head," she said to Henry. "Keep you from getting wet."

"I don't need it."

"You're not going to wear your hat, are you? You'll ruin it."

"No," said Henry, "I am not going to wear my hat. I have no desire to ruin it. But I don't think a few snowflakes will ruin my head."

"So you say, but you could get pneumonia in your silly head, and then I'd have to take care of you. It's always the women who have to tend the sick. And it's a lousy job and I don't want any part of it."

"Give me a blasted muffler," Henry said, and when she handed him one, he wound it around his head with vicious tugs. "I had hoped that you were not one of those women who always trap a man at the front door with a pair of rubbers and an umbrella."

"What's it to you if I am?"

"I don't quite know." He opened the door and went out, and she followed him.

There was more snow on the porch now, and it seemed to be falling more thickly than ever. The steps were almost obliterated, and Henry, gingerly feeling for the top one, found that the snow came up over the top of his storm boots. He turned and extended a hand to Diana but discovered that the gesture was unnecessary. She tripped over Claude's coat and made the short flight in one movement, landing head down in the snow at the bottom.

Henry said, "For God's sake, why can't you stay on your feet!" He jumped the remaining steps, and landed in snow up to his knees. He caught hold of Diana under the arms and pulled her to an upright position and then helped her to wipe snow from her indignant face.

"Now just shut up," she panted, as soon as she could talk. "I'll fall down if I want to."

"Take hold of the back of my coat," he said impatiently, "so that we'll stay together."

"Who wants to stay together?" she muttered sulkily.

He picked up the tail of his coat and handed it to her. "Here. Hang on and let's get going. It's coming down so heavily that any tracks will be obliterated very shortly."

They pressed on around the house and had to struggle through several deep drifts. Once or twice they stopped to examine what seemed to be a furrow, but decided each time that it had been caused by the wind.

Toward the back Diana moved in against the house to avoid a huge drift and stood leaning against the black clapboard on a little area of ground that the wind had blown almost bare. Her face was glowing with color and flakes of snow glistened in her vivid hair. She had closed her eyes, and Henry stood looking at her, tantalized by her beauty until she suddenly opened her eyes when he quickly turned his head away.

He moved over and looked through the window of the dining room, where they had placed Scrimmer. He was still where they had left him, sitting in the chair, but now Claude was seated opposite him and appeared to be talking to him.

Chapter 18

HENRY MOVED quickly away from the window, and Diana asked, "What is it?"

"Nothing. It's all right. I thought I saw something moving in there."

'But that's it. They're in there. They must be. You know those front doors don't shut all the way. They got in there, and they didn't know we were in the other side."

Henry shook his head. "We were just in there, and we looked through the whole place. They're not there."

Diana sighed. "How are we supposed to find them in all this mess of snow?"

Henry shrugged and began to fight his way around to the front again, while she plowed silently along behind him. They scrambled up the front steps and stamped some of the snow from their feet before they went in.

Diana removed Claude's coat and hung it on the rack. "Look," she said earnestly, "what did you find in that other house?"

Henry eyed her and then took a long breath. "All right, since you ask. We found Scrimmer there. He has been shot in the back side of his head. And he's very dead."

There was a startled feminine cry, but it did not come from Diana, who simply stared with round green eyes. Henry swung around in startled confusion and saw that Miss Robb stood at the foot of the stairs. She was neatly attired in a dark suit, wore no hat or coat, and appeared to be quite dry.

As Diana and Henry gaped at her, she composed herself and asked practically, "Who shot him?"

Henry blinked at her. "We don't know who shot him. How did you get in here?"

Miss Robb straightened her suit coat and said calmly, "We came in through the front door. It was unlocked, and since Mrs. Evans was very much fatigued after our experience with the young man who tried to drive his car sideways, I took the liberty of putting her to bed upstairs. I'd like to get her something to eat and some coffee. Is her husband is around?"

"How did you get in here without us knowing?" Henry asked, rumpling his hair.

"I'm sure I don't know." She had an air of impatience admirably controlled. "The door was not locked, and since I was concerned about Mrs. Evans, I simply helped her in and upstairs. I neither saw nor heard anyone."

"But I was in the hall," Diana said stupidly. "Oh, I suppose it must have been before— Did you go into the other house first?"

"I am afraid," said Miss Robb, still controlling impatience, "that I don't know what you're talking about. Is there coffee in the house? And some food?"

"I suppose so," Diana said absently. "I'll show you the kitchen. Who's Mrs. Evans?"

As they passed through the dining room, Ted gave Miss Robb a wary glance and became absorbed in his stockinged toes, but Claude rose out of his chair and yelled, "How in hell did you get out here?"

Miss Robb gave him a conservative nod, said, "Nasty weather, Mr. Boster," and disappeared into the kitchen behind Diana.

Claude turned on Ted and asked, "Did she come out with you?"

"As far as the lily pond," Ted admitted. "After that, she was on her own."

"Mrs. Evans is recovering in one of the bedrooms upstairs," Henry announced from the doorway.

Claude gave him a sharp glance and then sank back into his chair. "She's batty," he said heavily. "Evans must be back home by now." He stared down at his idle hands.

Henry stood looking at him and wondering. The old man must be batty himself, he thought, sitting in front of a dead man and talking to him. And he must have known that Scrimmer was out here at the house. No wonder he felt he had to come along. He'd hidden Scrimmer out here.

Henry walked over to the sideboard and got out the wine and some glasses. Ted watched him and presently let out a groan. "God help me, and I didn't bring any with me. Is that bilge all you have?"

Henry poured wine with a steady hand. "It's all we have, and if you suffer, it's no more than you deserve. Losing your temper and rushing out here, leaving your few patients sitting in the waiting room."

Ted took a long drink of the bilge and made a variety of derogatory noises. Henry sat down with his glass and found himself thinking about Scrimmer again. The thing wasn't at all clear. Evidently Scrimmer had come out here, with Evans detailed to show him the way. Yesterday, at about noon? But then who had fired those shots?

Claude said suddenly, "Can you cook?" and Henry looked up and saw that he was speaking to Ted. But as he looked at Claude's heavy red face he suddenly understood about the shots, and he felt like laughing. Only why laugh? By rights he ought to be furiously angry. Claude had fired those shots—fired to miss, certainly—so that the police would be assured that Scrimmer was still in town.

Ted was saying, "...and now that I'm dry, Henry, I want you to run me in to the nearest garage, so that I can get someone to come out and put my car on its feet again. Then you can get back to your hospital bed and I can get back to all my shining tools and get to work on you."

Henry laughed. "I can't get you to a garage. I'll face you in the right direction and give you a push."

Ted said urgently, "Henry, stop horsing around. I have to get back to town today. I have patients."

"Since when?"

"The only car out here," Claude said flatly, "that's still on its four feet is mine, and it's going to stay in the barn until the weather changes. If you want lunch, you'd better come out to the kitchen and help me cook it, or you won't get any."

Ted got to his feet. "I don't want any, chubby, not if you're going to cook it. I'm going back to town, even if I have to walk." He stalked out to the hall, and Henry followed and watched him as he put on his shoes and rubbers.

"Want some overshoes? We have an assortment here."

"No," said Ted coldly. "I might get a bill for them later."

"This was rather a trying trip for you to take just to call me names."

Ted opened the door and let in a gust of wind and snow. "I merely wanted to save your life," he said loftily, "but of course it doesn't matter."

"If you do get to town," Henry said mildly, "send the police out here. We need help."

Ted was looking gloomily out into the storm. He glanced back at Henry and muttered, "Certainly not. I shall send back a wagon with a couple of attendants and a straitjacket."

"If you were a doctor, you'd know that they don't use straitjackets any more. Listen, Ted, I'm not fooling. We need the police."

Ted trudged off into the snow without further words, and Henry turned back into the house. "Silly ass. If anyone gets my appendix it'll be somebody else."

In the hall he came face to face with Miss Robb, who bore a large tray in steady hands. It was loaded with food and coffee, and Henry sniffed with watering mouth. He said courteously, "I hope you've been able to make yourself comfortable. I'm glad you were able to come out."

She gave him a level look, said, "Please don't be absurd," and went on up the stairs. Henry gazed after her and impersonally admired her efficiency. She was a cool one, all right. He really ought to go up and see Mrs. Evans, but he'd let her enjoy her meal first in peace. Anyway, he was hardly a conventional host here any longer. He merely owned this haven for orphans of the storm. He thought again of the tray in Miss Robb's hands and went out to the kitchen in a hurry.

Claude had produced a tasty lunch for Diana and himself, and Henry hopefully pulled up a chair and sat down. Almost at once he got up again to get himself something to eat on and with.

"I didn't make anything for you," Claude said rudely.

"No," said Henry, "but, like all vain cooks, you always make too much, so there's plenty."

Diana giggled. "That girlfriend of yours, Miss Robb, is certainly on her toes, dashing all the way out here to see what you're up to."

Henry choked over his coffee and began indignantly, "She is not—"

But Claude interrupted with an evil grin, "Why d'ya want to deny it? Everybody knows the two of you have been bumbling around together for years. Time you married her, too. I have no time for a man who can't make up his sissy mind to take the plunge."

Hungry though he was, Henry laid his knife and fork down on the table and gave Claude a chilly eye. "You know perfectly well that it is Fred who has been casting sheep's eyes at Miss Robb. If you are trying to break up the romance which is beginning to flower between your daughter and myself by telling foul lies—"

Diana began to laugh hysterically, and after waiting for a moment Henry resumed his knife and fork and went back to his food.

Diana wiped her eyes and said weakly, "You'll just have to put up with me. I'm not myself. How could I be, anyway? I don't know what's going on, and nobody tells me anything."

Claude gave her a worried look. "Now, baby, you're not to bother about anything. I'm sorry about this mess, but I'll get you out of it. And long before the romance has a chance to bloom, too."

Henry swallowed a piece of potato and said, "What a dope."

"Where's that Ted?" Diana asked vaguely. "Doesn't he want lunch?"

"He went back to town in a huff."

Claude got up abruptly, said, "See that you do the dishes, Debbon," and left the room in what appeared to be a bit of a hurry.

Henry gazed after him speculatively. Was he returning to Scrimmer because Ted had departed and might conceivably send out the police? Ted had no knowledge of Scrimmer. Nobody had told him, but Claude didn't know that. Better follow him.

Henry stood up and found his way blocked by Diana, who handed him an apron with a stony face.

"You ate, too, and you'll do your share of the work."

Henry capitulated and assumed the apron. He discovered that Claude was a messy cook even though the results were good, and dirty pans were strewn over the length and breadth of the kitchen. Bits of food had been baked so firmly to the bottom of one pan that he had to use a chisel to free them.

Diana, who looked enchanting in a frilly apron, dried dishes with an abstracted look in her green eyes and occasionally brushed a strand of vivid hair from her forehead with the back of a bent wrist.

"Does Claude believe in spiritualism?" Henry asked, breaking a long silence.

"No, certainly not."

"Of course not, so why does he sit talking to a dead man?"

Diana fumbled at the half-dried dish in her hands and set it clattering onto the table.

"What do you mean?" she asked in a horrified whisper.

"Where is he now?"

"I don't know. How could I know?"

Henry removed his apron and wiped his hands on it. He went through to the front door, and Diana followed, her face white and scared. "You go and see," she said in a frightened voice. "Find out what he's doing. I—I'll wait here."

Henry went out onto the porch and pushed open the other door, and as it swung inward he heard a hoarse shout from the dining room.

Chapter 19

HENRY FORCED himself to walk into the hall, but he could feel the stirring of hair along his scalp. Someone was in there. It couldn't be Scrimmer who had yelled, because Scrimmer was dead. He certainly looked dead. He was dead. Perhaps it was Claude who had let out that hoarse cry.

But it wasn't Claude, and Scrimmer's body was still slumped, inert and remote, on the chair. It was Ted who stood there, trying to arrange his pallid features into the correct expression for a doctor viewing a corpse.

In the reaction from his fear, Henry became both peevish and scornful. "So that's the kind of crummy doctor you are, screaming at the sight of death. You ought to get a job in a school looking at the kids' tonsils."

Ted said haughtily, "I thought it was you, and knowing the condition of your appendix—"

"Never mind my appendix. Chances are, when you read that X-ray you were looking at your thumb on the edge of the negative. What are you doing in here, anyway?"

"The storm was too much for me, so I came back, but you were so inhospitable that I thought I'd camp in here and not bother you."

Diana came up behind Henry, and he swung around quickly. "Don't come in here. You wouldn't want to see it."

Her eyes widened in horror, but she turned back without protest.

"I don't want to see him, either," Ted declared, making for the hall. "It gave me a nasty shock, I can tell you, coming on him sitting there like that."

Henry barred his way. "You go back in there and look him over. I want to know how long he's been dead."

"For God's sake, can't it wait? I'm all wet."

"So you are," Henry agreed, "and have been as long as I've known you."

"I'm also hungry. And who's going to pay me for making this examination?"

"I wouldn't care to commit myself on that, but I can assure you that you'll get no lunch until it's done."

Ted stamped back into the dining room, and after a brief and what appeared to be a sketchy examination of the body, said sulkily, "He was shot."

"You don't mean it! I thought it was measles. How long has he been dead?"

Ted stooped over the body again, and presently announced with simplicity, "I don't know."

"Can't you make a stab at it?"

"You can't bluff in medicine the way you can in law," Ted said peevishly. "I don't want to go on record—"

"Where's the record? I merely want an opinion as between us boys."

"Oh, well, only a short time."

"Do you mean two short days or two short hours?"

"Hours, you dumb oaf. Maybe two, or less or more. How do I know? I wasn't here. Did you shoot him? Is that why you wanted the police? To give yourself up? What did you want to shoot him for, anyway?"

"If I'd shot him," Henry said patiently, "I wouldn't have had to ask you how long he'd been dead, because I would have known. Simple arithmetical calculation."

"Can't we get some lunch?" Ted asked. "I'm starving. Do you mean to say you don't know who shot him? What about the red-haired babe, or old chubby?"

"She is not a babe," Henry said coldly, "and she hasn't shot anyone."

They walked down the hall to the front door, and Ted asked, "Are you making a play for this redhead? I mean, the corny, gallant defense stuff seems to indicate it."

"What's it to you?"

They went into the other side of the house, and Ted murmured, "Ah! Warmth again! About the girl—if you really care, Debbon, I shall step aside and clear the way for you. After all, I'm no hog."

"I'll have to take your word for it," Henry said furiously, "since you certainly look like one. And don't bother stepping aside for me. I do my best work when I have competition, even if it's poor competition like you."

"O.K., brother, don't say I didn't make the gesture. And you'll see how poor the competition is."

He went back to the kitchen, and at the same time Diana started down the stairs.

"Papa's up there," she said to Henry, "in the bathroom. Is that Ted man trying to get himself something to eat?"

Henry scowled. "Leave him alone. He's very uncouth when he's hungry."

"I think you're positively rude to him," she said, and went off to the kitchen.

Henry took a step after her and then changed his mind and went up the stairs instead, impelled by a dutiful urge to say a few courteous words to Mrs. Evans.

He found her lying on Diana's bed, while Miss Robb sat on a chair, smoking a cigarette. Mrs. Evans had removed her shoes, and when Henry came in, she wiggled her toes uncomfortably in their sensible stockings, as though she felt they should be covered.

"Mr. Debbon," she said in a distressed voice, "where is my poor husband?"

"I'm sorry, I don't know. Haven't you any idea of where he went?"

She shook her head. "It's been such a shock. I just had a note from him, saying he was away on confidential business. See, he didn't come home at all night before last, and yesterday I didn't hear from him, so today I went to the office, and there was that young doctor fellow looking for you, and Miss Robb simply frantic because Mr. Boster hadn't been in, so—"

"So," observed Claude from the doorway, "you came out with the young doctor fellow, leaving the office entirely unguarded."

He was looking at Miss Robb, but she took the indictment with the utmost aplomb. She said composedly, "Our efficient office girl is in charge, and we could have no one more to the point, at the moment, since she doesn't know enough to answer any questions."

Claude stuck a cigar into the corner of his mouth and chewed vigorously on it. "O.K., maybe you know what you mean by that, but will you kindly come into my room, so that we can talk without the annoyance of flapping ears in the vicinity?"

He took Miss Robb by the arm, led her through the connecting door, and shut it behind him with a resounding bang.

"Oh, dear!" Mrs. Evans moaned. "That poor girl!" Henry, staring at the closed door, realized that Miss Robb knew all of Claude's business and felt distinct twinges of jealousy. He knew very little of the old man's affairs himself, but of course Miss Robb had been in the firm longer and was Claude's private secretary

It had become quite dark, and Henry went over and switched on the light. He glanced at his watch and was astonished to discover that it was close to five o'clock.

Mrs. Evans raised herself, swung her legs off the bed, and stood up. She was short and rather heavy and had iron gray hair that was twisted into a knot, which had begun to slip. She walked to the bureau and began nervously to take hairpins out and put them in again.

"If he's not here," she said unhappily, "I'll have to go back, because he might have returned home, and what would he do if I'm not there to take care of him?"

"I'm afraid it won't be possible for you to leave until the storm is over," Henry said courteously.

"Oh, I must, really. Now, where did that girl put my coat?"

"You won't need your coat," Henry said, still courteous, but adding a little firmness to it. "We can't get the car out, and certainly you cannot walk. I'm afraid you'll have to make up your mind to stay, for a while, at least."

"But, Mr. Debbon," she protested, her voice almost a wail, "I can't just stay in this room. I'm thoroughly rested now, and I—I must do something."

"Come on down to the dining room," Henry suggested. "It's warm and comfortable, and you can talk to the others or I'll find you a book to read."

Mrs. Evans had stepped into her neat oxfords and was busy tying neat utilitarian bows over her instep. She got up with a sigh and followed Henry out into the hall, and he said cordially, "It gets so dark these winter days."

It was the right approach. Mrs. Evans said, with more animation than she had yet displayed, "It certainly does, indeed."

Henry switched on the light in the hall and led the way downstairs. He extended a hand backward to help Mrs. Evans, but his mind was on Scrimmer. If Ted were right, the poor wretch had been killed only that morning. After they were up, in fact.

The dining-room light was on, and he could hear Diana and Ted chatting in there. He led Mrs. Evans forward, but just as they approached the entrance all the lights went out.

Chapter 20

HENRY STOOD still and felt his heart sink. The lights out here were always apt to fail during a storm, and it might be days before they came on again, especially during a storm as bad as this one.

He heard Mrs. Evans say behind him, "Oh, dear, oh, dear, what on earth has happened?" and from the dining room Diana called in an annoyed voice, "Who did that?" Ted yelled, "Henry! Come and get the candles!"

Henry felt for Mrs. Evans's arm, found it, and led her into the dining room. He guided her to a chair and lowered her into it. She sank obediently but wailed, "I'm scared in the dark like this. Can't we have some light?"

Diana asked, "Is that you, Henry?

"I don't know," he said bitterly. "I can't see in the dark."

"Isn't he a card?" Ted's voice asked. "Henry, for the love of God, get the candles out. They're right in the sideboard here, where Auntie always kept them."

"Why don't you get them yourself, if you know so much about where Auntie always kept them?" Henry demanded.

"Because I've got my coffee cup halfway to my mouth, and I have to keep it there as I don't know where the saucer is or where my mouth is, you silly fool!"

Henry groped and eventually found candles and lit one. Diana produced a couple of candlesticks, and Ted was at last able to get his suspended coffee cup to his mouth.

Henry regarded him sourly and asked, "How does he get to eat in the dining room, when the rest of us have to pig it in the kitchen?"

Ted set down his coffee cup and explained, "I was raised very particular. I've never et in the kitchen in my life."

"Wait until our cook gets dinner," Henry said loftily. "You'll find you haven't et at all, if you haven't et in the kitchen."

Mrs. Evans moaned, "Oh, dear, oh, dear, how can we do any cooking with no light?"

Henry let out a few quiet curses, and Diana said crossly, "What's the matter with you now? Why can't you at least be cheerful when we have such troubles?"

"Certainly. Of course. Will you accompany me to the cellar, dear, while I look for kindling wood to light the kitchen range? As you have no doubt observed, the electricity has failed, but to start a fire in the range in your company will be pure pleasure."

"Pure apple sauce," Ted observed. "Don't you go with him, baby. He'll serve you with some sort of paper as sure as hell."

"All right," Henry said, with assured indifference. "Stay here and wash up his dirty dishes."

Mrs. Evans moaned, "Oh, dear, oh, dear!"

Diana stood up. "For heavens' sake, let's go and light the kitchen range so that Papa can roast his leg of lamb."

"Lamb!" Mrs. Evans exclaimed, and looked really alert for the first time. "Merciful heavens! If it's lamb, it should certainly be in the oven right now!"

Henry went into the front hall and searched among the galoshes for a flashlight, which he felt sure was there and which he eventually found. He returned to the dining room and nodded to Diana. "Come on, let's go."

She followed him down to the cellar, and he found an old grocery box which he mangled into kindling wood while Diana held the flashlight. He started a fire in the kitchen range and carefully built it up with coal, and presently Mrs. Evans came out from the dining room, bearing a candle and interested in progress.

Henry remembered Miss Robb and Claude, still upstairs and apparently in the dark. He went back into the dining room, where Ted was still eating. He lit a candle and went on out into the hall, calling over his shoulder, "Greedy pig!"

Miss Robb and Claude had groped their way to the head of the stairs, and Claude was no longer in possession of his temper.

"So here you are!" he yelled furiously. "I should have thought that common courtesy would have sent you up with some light when you knew that we were stuck in a strange house in the dark."

"Oh, shut it off!" Henry said wearily. "This house isn't strange to you. You visited my aunt out here before I was born."

"Any time I visited your blasted aunt," Claude fumed, "was on business that I never should have bothered with—once in twenty years. The only other time was that infernal house party that you gave, thinking to further yourself in the firm. Why do you think I should know the ins and outs of this sagging old wreck?"

Henry jammed his candle into a candlestick that was standing on a table and said, "There! Now you'd better get down to your cooking. I think Mrs. Evans is taking an interest, and her ideas may not coincide with yours." He went on into the bedrooms to distribute candles, while Claude and Miss Robb descended the stairs.

When they walked into the dining room Ted ignored Claude and stood up, eying Miss Robb. He gave a rather flourishing bow and asked, "Will you have a seat, young lady?"

Miss Robb raised her eyebrows. "We seem to have become fairly amiable all of a sudden. As for the seat, I have a nice one and don't need another." However, she went over to him, plucked a cigarette from his pocket, and lit it at the candle.

Claude asked, "Where is that damned interfering Evans woman?" and went through to the kitchen, where he found her bending over the range. Diana was at the sink, peeling potatoes.

"What's going on here?" Claude demanded. "It's too early to put the meal on yet."

Mrs. Evans raised a flushed face and said briskly, "Now, just you get out of here. I can't tolerate men in the kitchen when I'm cooking."

"I beg your, pardon, madam," Claude said, drawing himself up, "but—"

Diana dusted her hands and sighed. "There! That's done! Come on, Papa." She took him back into the dining room, where Henry was lighting more candles. Ted and Miss Robb had disappeared.

"Let's have some wine," Diana suggested.

Henry poured three glasses and then picked up his flashlight and stuffed it into his pocket. "Don't want this stolen from me now," he observed.

Claude said, "These glasses are the height of ill taste," and held up his to have it refilled.

"Papa, please!" Diana protested. "You shouldn't have any more."

"I haven't had much, baby. And I need it."

Henry filled his glass, and then drank off his own and refilled that.

Diana scowled at both of them and said, "Neither one of you knows how to drink wine. It should be sipped."

"Where have you been all this time?" Claude asked Henry.

"I had a few odd jobs to attend to. Things that you, as a gentleman, could hardly be asked to do."

Diana got up with an impatient gesture and went to the window, where she stood staring moodily out into the snow.

"Do you know," she said presently, "I believe it's stopped snowing, although it's too dark to be sure."

Henry went to stand beside her and played the flashlight against the pane. The snow had stopped falling, but a high wind had come up and was whirling the flakes in crazy circles around the yard. It screamed around the corners of the house, and Claude said from behind them, "I loathe these old shacks that always start wailing in a wind."

A particularly violent gust swept across the yard, and as it subsided, Diana gave a frightened little cry. Directly in the path of light from the flash, and uncovered by the recent gust of wind, they saw a man's hat and an arm lying in the snow.

Chapter 21

HENRY CLICKED off the flashlight and said grimly, "I'll have to go out and get him."

"What is it?" Claude demanded, his voice shaking. "What's out there? What are you looking at?"

"Oh, God, Papa!" Diana moaned. "It's a man. He's out there in the snow, half buried."

Henry had already gone out to the hall and was pulling on his overshoes. Claude followed him and reached silently for his coat, and Diana cried, "Wait till I go upstairs. My coat's up in my room."

Henry, shrugging into his coat, gave her a doubtful glance.

"I don't think you'd better come, although of course one of you will have to help me."

"I'm coming," Claude said briefly. "You stay here, baby."

Diana stopped halfway up the stairs and looked at him rebelliously. "No, no, I don't want to."

"Baby, please! Do as I say just this once."

She came down again reluctantly and said in a scared voice, "I don't like being left here like this."

Henry clicked the flashlight on and off to make sure that it was working, and Claude muttered, "For God's sake, come on, will you? Man freezing to death out there while you play with your toys."

Diana called, "Please don't be long," and closed the door after them, and they began to struggle through the heaped-up snow on the steps.

The going was bad. The wind howled at them and flung particles of stinging snow against their faces as they pushed through the drifts. Henry went first, leading the way around the side of the house and playing the flashlight ahead. Claude fought along behind him, cursing when he had breath and stumbling frequently. Once he fell, and Henry turned back and helped him to his feet. He noticed that he wore light shoes and said impatiently, "I should think that even you would have sense enough to put on overshoes for a job like this."

"How in the name of hell am I going to put on overshoes when I haven't got any damned blasted overshoes?" Claude shouted furiously.

"I could have fixed you up if you'd taken the trouble to use your tongue for something besides swearing."

They were opposite the dining-room window now and could see a blurred outline of Diana, with the faint flicker of the candle behind her. Henry stopped and played the flashlight around, but there was no longer any sign of the hat or the arm, and he realized that the wind had shifted the snow. He called to Claude to stay where he was and began to move cautiously in what he thought was the right direction, but Claude ignored his order and panted along behind him. Sometimes the snow was up over their knees, and again it merely whirled around their ankles, and when the gusts of wind became too savage, they had to stand with their backs to it and wait until it subsided. After each gust Henry played the flashlight around in the hope that the hat or arm would be uncovered again, until Claude yelled in complete exasperation, "Stop playing and dig for him, you stupid ass!"

Henry, chilled to the bone already, stiffened further and began, "I am not a—" when a particularly violent wind blew the words from his lips. He heard Claude struggling for breath and began to be afraid that he'd have to get him back to the house before he attempted the other job. He thought, impatiently, that he should have brought Diana with him. She was young and strong and better able to stand up to an undertaking of this sort. He took Claude's arm and tried to urge him in the direction of the house, but Claude flung him off angrily.

He played the flashlight around again and saw at once that the body was almost at his feet, only this time it was the legs that were uncovered. Henry dropped to his knees and began furiously to brush the snow away until he had bared the face, and then he saw that it was

Evans. The body was stiff—frozen—and Henry felt quite certain that the man was dead.

He heard an odd whistling sigh behind him and turned to find Claude down in the snow. He eased an arm under his shoulders and tried to raise him, and Claude muttered jerkily, "I'm all right. Let me get my breath."

Henry returned to Evans and began to drag him in the direction of the house. It was very difficult, but he made slow progress and had covered a certain amount of the distance when he saw another figure approaching and presently recognized it as Diana. He turned the flashlight on her and saw that she was wrapped up like a mummy in mufflers and that she was shivering violently.

"Oh, what is it?" she asked in a quavering voice. "Who—who is he?"

"It's Evans. I'm glad you came. We'll have to get Mr. Boster back to the house. He's lying in the snow over there."

Diana drew in her breath sharply, and then they saw that Claude was on his feet again and was making his way slowly and painfully toward them. They closed in on each side of him and took his arms, and he walked along between them, silent, except for his heavy breathing. They took him back into the house, and by that time he seemed to have recovered a little. He shook Henry's hand from his arm and said desperately, "Go and get Evans. He's still alive. He *must* be still alive."

"I think he's dead," Henry said flatly.

"He can't be. He isn't. I just saw him. Go and get him, will you?"

Henry went out again, and found that this time the journey was easier, since he could use the tracks that they had just made. He managed to get Evans to the foot of the porch steps, and then Diana appeared again and silently helped him to get the stiff body up to the porch. Henry was heading for the door to the other side of the house, but Diana stopped him,

"No, no, Papa is waiting for him. We—we'll have to take him into our side until Papa is sure he's dead."

Claude was waiting just inside the door as Diana and Henry staggered in with their burden. They dropped the body to the floor, and Claude said excitedly, "Not here. Bring him into the dining room and put him on the couch."

"He's going next door with the other one," Henry said briefly. "Here, take the flashlight and examine him. There's nothing to be done for him now."

Claude bent over the stiff figure and looked into the face, while Diana turned her head away. When he raised himself at last his cheeks seemed to have fallen in, and Henry had the curious feeling that he was someone else. There was a short silence, and then Claude said hopelessly, "All right, we'll take him in there."

"Not you, Papa," Diana protested. "Henry and I can do it."

"No, no, no. Certainly not," Claude cried agitatedly. "It's no job for a delicate young girl. You'll only get cold, and you're shivering now. I'm all right. Henry and I can do it."

Henry took the flashlight again and thought resignedly that he had never known Ted to be around when he was most needed. He said, "We'll have to get Mrs. Evans and Ted. I'll take him into the other house."

Diana dropped her eyes and twisted her hands unhappily. "I simply can't go and tell her. I thought it would be best to take him in there and then break it to her gently."

"No." Henry was firm. "You'll have to do it, and Mr. Boster should be with you."

Claude snorted. "Don't you start pointing out my duty, you half-witted ambulance chaser!"

"Come on, Papa," Diana said resignedly. "Henry's right. I'll have to tell her, and you were his employer, so you should be with me. We'll break it to her, and then we'll let her come out and see him, although he doesn't look very—er—"

She took Claude's arm firmly and led him away, while he bleated feebly, "But, baby, I don't actually see why—I mean, why should we—?"

They disappeared into the kitchen, where Mrs. Evans was presumably still wrestling with the dinner.

Henry called, "Ted!" and then stooped over and took off his galoshes. There was no reply, but he could hear voices raised in joke and laughter coming from the second floor. He called again—more peremptorily—and Ted came to the head of the stairs and was immediately joined by Miss Robb. They sat down together on the top step.

"You're getting to be somewhat of a bore, Henry," Ted said, yawning. "What do you want now? Is the place on fire, or is dinner ready?"

"Stop assing around," Henry said urgently, "and listen! The body of Mr. Evans is down here, and you'd better come and have a look at it."

Ted looked at him, obviously puzzled, but Miss Robb rose to her feet and clattered down the stairs. She gasped, "Evans! Where is he?"

Ted started after her slowly, and as she caught sight of the body, she sank to her knees beside it and whispered, "Oh, my God!"

Henry looked at Ted. "Where the devil have you been?"

"I've been showing Miss Robb the upper part of this peculiar house." He glanced down at the body and added, "God almighty! Another? Who killed this one?"

Henry ran frantic fingers through his hair and muttered, "How the hell do I know? Look him over and find out what killed him, will you?"

Ted dropped to his knees, made a cursory examination, and presently announced, "As far as I can see, nothing killed him."

"Then I suppose he's still alive," Henry snarled.

Ted straightened up. "You don't suppose anything of the silly kind. He's frozen stiff. But what happened to him before the freeze is something to be determined."

"Then suppose you show a return on the money your unfortunate parents spent on your education and determine it."

"Get him onto a table," Ted said, dusting off his hands, "or a couch will do, and remove his clothes, and I'll see what I can give you on it."

"Do you want a bust in the nose?" Henry asked quietly. "You—"

"Hush, both of you!" Miss Robb turned outraged eyes on them. "Where's Mrs. Evans? This is a mess—it's really bad. Does Mr. Boster know of it?"

A shrill cry from the kitchen seemed to indicate that Mrs. Evans had been told, and a moment later she came running through the hall and dropped to her knees beside the body. They allowed her to crouch there for a while, and then Diana and Miss Robb raised her with firm hands and took her upstairs.

Ted and Henry carried Evans into the other house, while Claude held the flashlight and opened doors. He insisted that they put the body in the front room instead of taking it back to the dining room, and Henry felt as though a cold finger were tracing a line down the middle of his back. Claude, he thought hysterically, didn't want the dead Evans to listen to what he had to say to the dead Scrimmer.

"I'll come back and look him over later," Ted said grimly. "I'd better go up now and see what I can do for Mrs. Evans." They went back to the other side, and Diana came down the stairs as Ted went up. She followed Henry and Claude into the dining room and watched apathetically while Claude poured wine for himself with an unsteady hand. He sank into an armchair, and Henry had just picked up a glass for himself when there was a loud knocking at the front door.

Chapter 22

CLAUDE ROSE up out of his chair and whispered, "Don't answer it—don't—"

"Pull yourself together," Henry said shortly. "Of course I'll answer it. Someone lost in the storm, probably." He squared his shoulders, marched out into the hall, and found himself wondering whether Diana was admiring his courage, but when he got to the front door he paused and pulled out Claude's gun and then was somewhat taken aback to find that Diana was right behind him.

"Get back into the dining room," he said peremptorily.

"No."

Henry pushed her behind the door as he opened it and stepped back himself. He pointed the gun at the aperture and said, "Who's there?" He had intended using a low, firm voice, and was astounded to hear the words come out in a high squeak. Diana giggled nervously.

There was a moment of silence, and then a man stepped into the hall and said composedly, "Even if that's a water pistol, I wish you'd point it at the floor. I'm plenty wet already."

It was Gilling.

Henry hoped that his flooding relief was not too obvious. He pocketed the gun again and asked, "How did you find us?"

"It was not easy," Gilling said severely. "I still don't understand why you didn't tell me where you were going."

"I didn't think you'd be interested."

"Oh," Diana said. "It's that policeman."

"I'm not a policeman. I was promoted."

"That's nice," Diana murmured vaguely. "Congratulations. When did it happen?"

"Thank you," said Gilling. "Ten years ago."

He walked toward the flickering light in the dining room, and the other two followed him. Claude had disappeared, and Gilling sank into his vacated chair and murmured exhaustedly, "I'd like a little scotch, if you don't mind." Henry poured some wine, and Diana clicked her tongue.

"You must be simply dead, fighting your way here through all that snow."

"I would never have attempted it if I had known," Gilling replied and divided an accusing look between them. "The bus is not running. Some fellow gave me a lift in a sleigh until his horse got tired of it all, and then he gave me directions. I have been walking for some hours."

He picked up the glass of wine and gave it a stricken look.

Henry shrugged. "It's all we have. Sorry."

Claude came back into the room, glared at Gilling, and asked, "What are you doing here?"

Gilling merely raised an eyebrow at him and then drank the wine,

Claude found another chair and perched on the edge of it, looking uncomfortable and aggrieved, and Henry asked, "Didn't you bring anyone with you? We need help here."

"You need help," Gilling repeated flatly. "You all came out here without a word to me, and I had to guess where you'd gone. Even then I didn't know. If I'd guessed wrong, and you hadn't been here with some warmth and this revolting wine, I'd probably have died of exposure."

"If you'll pardon me," Claude said, "I'll just bust into tears at the bare thought. Wad'ya chasing us for, anyway? You were supposed to be looking for Scrimmer."

"Wherever you are Scrimmer seems to be also," Gilling said coldly.

"D'ya mean you think we have him here with us?"

"Yes." Gilling extended his glass to Henry. "More poison, please."

Henry took the glass and stood holding it and looking at Gilling. "What makes you think we have him here?"

Gilling looked up at him. "Where is he? Hiding?"

"No." Henry picked up the wine bottle. "He's dead."

There was a blank silence while Gilling looked first at Claude and then at Henry, who handed him the refilled glass.

"You'd better not have too much of that stuff until you eat something," Diana suggested practically.

Gilling looked at her and then down at his glass. "Yes," he muttered abstractedly. "I'm hungry."

"If you think I'm going to cook for him too," Claude said furiously, "you'd better start thinking again."

Henry glanced at his watch. "We all need something to eat. But there are a lot of things I want to get cleared up. I don't like this confusion."

"It's too damned bad about what you don't like," Claude snorted. "I'm hungry, too, but I'm tired. You and Diana go and get some sort of a lousy meal together. Maybe Gilling can explain everything to you when he's been fed. Go on now. I'm an old man, and I've had all I can take."

Diana stood up at once and said, "Come on, Henry," and he followed her out of the room. They went to the kitchen, where Diana opened the door of the refrigerator and stared rather aimlessly inside.

Henry peered over her shoulder. "Not much there. It's lucky that a face-stuffer like your dear brother Fred is on the ocean, instead of being one of us."

She turned around to frown at him. "I have no brother, Henry Debbon, and I won't have you calling that—that—"

"Trifler? Wastrel? Buffoon? Dolt?"

"Well Anyway, he isn't my brother and you're not to say he is." She turned back to the refrigerator, and added after a moment, "Of course Papa adores Fred, so I suppose he must have something."

"What, for instance?"

"Oh, do shut up!" She snatched a dish from the refrigerator and banged it onto the table.

Henry went quietly into the butler's pantry and laid his ear against the door.

"—can't see any other explanation," Claude was saying. "Evans always did use his head too much, so in the end it wore out before he did, and he went nuts. Killed Scrimmer and then went outside and did away with himself."

"Oh?" said Gilling unemotionally. "How did he do it? Shoot himself?"

"Well, I—we don't know. Didn't examine him. We have nothing but candles and a flashlight."

"Was there a gun in his hand or in the snow close to him?"

"I—I don't know. Perhaps it's on him somewhere. We didn't look."

"I doubt if he would have put it back in his pocket after shooting himself."

"Oh, for God's sake!" Claude exclaimed. "The damn blasted gun may be lying out in the snow. I tell you we couldn't look. And he was all huddled up, anyway."

"Where is he?" Gilling asked. "I'll have to have a look at him."

"In the other side of the house. It's unoccupied. Henry's mad aunt divided the place up into two."

"I'll go in now."

Gilling stood up, and Henry backed silently into the kitchen.

Diana pushed red hair back from her face and said crossly, "Where have you been? I won't do this all alone."

Unexpectedly, Gilling walked into the kitchen, and as Henry whirled around he asked, "Have you got the keys to the other side of the house?"

"Yes, but I won't give them up. I'll go with you."

"Why won't you give them up?"

"Never mind. I just won't."

Gilling shrugged, and they went together to the front hall.

"Better put your coat on," Henry said. "It's cold in there."

They both put coats on, and Gilling followed Henry out to the porch and to the other door. Henry pushed it, and they went into the cold hall and to the living room, where Henry played the flashlight on the sofa where Evans's body lay.

Gilling made a long and careful investigation, and Henry watched intently. There was no weapon in any of the pockets, and there did not appear to be any wound on the body.

Gilling straightened up at last and said, "Heart attack, perhaps. If so, that might clear things up. He shot Scrimmer, and then ran out in a panic. Had an attack out in the snow and died where he fell."

"Maybe. But why did he kill Scrimmer? And he must have used Scrimmer's own gun to do the killing. Evans would never have a gun of his own."

"Details," said Gilling indifferently. "We have Scrimmer and his killer. Now all we have to do is to get back to civilization. Tomorrow, I hope."

Henry turned back into the hall. "I'm glad you're satisfied, but we definitely heard footsteps on the stairs after Evans must have been lying out in the snow."

"Don't be difficult," Gilling said cheerfully.

"All right, button it up and feel smug about it. But there's someone else hanging around here. Besides the other three, I mean."

Gilling allowed a certain amount of irritability to creep into his voice. "How many people are hanging around this Godforsaken place in a howling blizzard? A convention?"

"Mr. Boster thought this would be a good place for Scrimmer to hide out," Henry said. "At least that's the way I see it. He sent Evans with him to bring him out here and show him the way. When I decided to come out here, unexpectedly, Mr. Boster had to come, too, because he knew they were here. He was badly upset when he found Scrimmer dead."

Gilling grunted as they came out onto the porch, and for a moment they stood there, looking out over the expanse of snow. The wind had dropped, and a white moon glittered in the cold sky.

"Come on," Gilling muttered. "I've seen enough snow to last me for the rest of my life."

They went back into the house and removed their coats. There was no one in the dining room, but sounds from the kitchen seemed to indicate that Claude had decided to lend a hand with the dinner after all.

Gilling dropped into Claude's chair, and Henry sat opposite him and asked at once, "Did you find out who was shooting at me?"

"At the young lady, you mean."

"Not at the young lady," Henry said firmly. "I was the target."

"Scrimmer."

"Scrimmer came straight out here with Evans. There are several things to prove that. As a matter of fact ,I think it was Boster. He had no intention of hitting me, but he wanted it to appear that Scrimmer was still in town, after he'd sent him out here."

"Why?"

"What do you mean, 'why'?" Henry demanded.

"Why all the elaboration?"

"Well." Henry frowned into the candlelight. "I think Roster had some sort of a deal on with Scrimmer."

Gilling nodded. "He did. Scrimmer had a lot of money, which he'd hidden. Boster needs it now, and he was trying to get it."

Diana came into the dining room and looked from one to the other of them. "Where's Papa?"

"Thought he was in the kitchen with you," Gilling said, without much interest.

Henry got up and went quickly into the hall. He slipped on his coat and crept into the other house. It was very dark, but there was a faint glimmer of light from the dining room, and Henry tiptoed along the hall and cautiously peered in.

Claude held the one candle in his hand, and he was seated opposite the figure of Scrimmer.

"I'll bring you some food later," he was saying in a low voice, "but you must tell me where the money is."

Chapter 23

CLAUDE STOOD UP, and Henry moved back, quickly and quietly. He slipped into the living room, and Claude presently emerged, walked down the hall, and went out the front door, closing it behind him.

Henry went back to the dining room. He could see, dimly, the figure of Scrimmer in the chair, and after a moment he turned away. The dining room was noticeably warmer than the living room, and he thought that perhaps he'd better get Gilling to help him move Scrimmer in with Evans. As for Claude, it appeared that the sooner they got him into a sanitarium, the better.

He went out the front door, closed it after him, and slowly went back into the other house.

In the dining room Claude was sitting in his usual chair and Gilling was stretched out on the sofa, fast asleep. Henry went on to the kitchen, where Diana turned to him and with an oddly defensive note in her voice said, "The dinner's cooked."

"Good. I'm starving."

Diana sighed. "That's a shame. I was hoping you wouldn't be hungry. Because when I said cooked, I mean really cooked. Maybe it's the stove, but I never saw things go brown and even black quite so quickly. And yet you wouldn't want to eat the stuff raw, would you?"

Henry echoed her sigh and went and stuck his head into the dining room. "Mr. Boster," he said, "would you mind coming in and putting the finishing touches to the dinner?"

Claude gave him a suspicious look and then heaved himself to his feet. In the kitchen he surveyed Diana's efforts and then said mildly, "Get a little butter, baby."

Diana brought butter, and Claude dropped large chunks into every dish and then added salt and pepper. "Always remember, baby," he said, "that if the food hasn't turned out too well in the cooking, melted butter and seasoning will do wonders."

"You're so clever, Papa," she said admiringly.

They put the food on the table, and Henry went and woke Gilling.

Gilling came back from his dreams reluctantly and peevishly, but Henry was firm. "You should eat something. Chances are you'll be up most of the night. Claude's gone off his nut."

Gilling rubbed a closed fist across his eyes and muttered, "What makes you think so?"

"He keeps going into the other side of the house and talking to Scrimmer's dead body."

Gilling gave a prodigious yawn, which ended in a groan. "O.K., let's eat. We'll have a talk after dinner."

In the kitchen Claude and Diana were already seated at the table, eating the well-cooked dinner. Claude looked up at them, and then said to Diana, with something of defiance in his voice, "It's delicious, baby. You're a born cook."

Diana patted his arm. "Now, Papa, you know perfectly well it's just that butter and stuff you put in that makes it nice."

Gilling slipped into a chair and started to help himself, and Henry asked, "Where are the rest of us going to sit?"

Claude growled, "Who cares?"

"Well"—Diana wrinkled her forehead—"I expect it will have to be a sort of buffet."

"I suppose I'm confused because I'm so tired," Gilling observed.

"Are there others? Live ones, I mean?"

Henry nodded. "Mrs. Evans, Miss Robb, and a misfit who got an M.D. owing to influence in high places."

"Where are they?"

"As soon as I've finished," Diana explained, "I'm going up to look after Mrs. Evans, and then they can come down and eat."

Gilling nodded. "I'll go up with you. Perhaps I can get some information out of her."

Claude gave him an ugly side glance. "Be sure and eat up all you can, so there'll be nothing left for the others."

Henry picked up a plate and helped himself to some of the diminishing supplies. Diana and Gilling finished their meal and left, and Claude moved restlessly. "Seems to me she must have spilled something in the oven," he said, frowning. "I can smell it."

Henry got up and opened the oven door and gave a low whistle. "Look at that," he said, indicating a pan which contained a browned leg of lamb surrounded by succulently browned potatoes. "Mrs. Evans must have done this earlier. There'll be enough for everyone, after all. In fact, I think I'll have some myself."

Claude exploded out of his chair with a red face. "These blasted, infernal women!" he raved. "Think they can cook! Look at that lovely leg. One of the best I've ever seen and she's had it in there for hours! Ruined. Cooked to a rag—the best leg I've had for months!"

Henry pulled the pan out of the oven and put it on top of the stove. "Rag or no rag," he murmured, "it looks good."

He cut a few slices and offered some to Claude, who refused in thoroughly offensive language. "I think you're making a mistake," Henry said mildly and began to eat with enjoyment. He added, "It's odd that Diana didn't notice this."

Miss Robb and Ted came in, and while Ted helped himself to food, Miss Robb arranged a tray for Mrs. Evans. "Eating again already?" Henry asked.

Ted said, "Don't apologize. I know things have been a bit upset, but of course you're doing your best."

Claude was scowling at Miss Robb. "I hope you don't expect to get paid for this vacation of yours."

"Time and a half," she said firmly.

"You call this a vacation that the poor girl is having?" Henry demanded.

Claude shifted his eyes. "As for you, you're fired without references."

Miss Robb deposited a cup and saucer on her tray and said, "Oh, no, he isn't. Henry is my new boyfriend."

Ted stopped chewing and stared, and Henry said hastily, "Now listen, Robby, this is no time to get funny."

"I'm not being funny. I heard that you have a secret yearning for me, and I've decided to smile on your suit."

Ted looked slightly puzzled. "I suppose you're joking, but if you happen to be serious and decide to take him, I hope you'll spruce him up a little."

Miss Robb left the room with the tray in her competent hands, and Claude got up and lumbered out after her.

"Did you tell that Robb that I was sweet on her?" Henry asked ominously.

Ted swallowed lamb and said severely, "Can't you, in this house of death, keep your wretched love affairs for a more appropriate time and place? You babble of being sweet on girls when I am steeling myself to go in and determine how this Evans died."

"How and when."

"Why this emphasis on 'when' all the time? It's irritating."

"Of course it's irritating," Henry agreed, "for a man of your limited capabilities, but do the best you can."

Ted had finished his meal and he stood up, settled his tie, and left the room with measured tread. Henry, left alone, looked around gloomily at the mess of dirty pans and dishes. He picked up a few of the plates that were nearest to him and took them to the sink, where he began to wash them under the running faucet.

Miss Robb came in and said, "I don't see why you wash the dishes before I've even started to eat."

Henry dropped a half-washed plate into the sink and turned off the faucet. He watched Miss Robb assemble a meal for herself, and then poured coffee for both of them and sat down at the table with her.

"Now look, Robby, why are you telling people that I'm your boyfriend?"

She finished chewing, swallowed, and said calmly, "My boyfriend Fred has gone to Europe, so I need a replacement, and I thought you'd do."

Henry looked at her. "No," he said. "No, I won't do at all."

"Oh?"

"Even so. Now tell me, what did Gilling get out of Mrs. Evans?"

"You mean that fat little hairless policeman that turned up out of nowhere?"

"Yes. Were you there when he talked to Mrs. Evans?"

Miss Robb nodded. "He did quite a lot of talking, as a matter of fact."

"What did Mrs. Evans say?"

Miss Robb sighed. "Mostly, she just said over and over, 'Oh, my poor husband.'"

"That all?"

"Well, right at the end she threatened to throw everything in the room at his ugly bald head if he didn't get out and leave her alone."

Henry suppressed a grin and asked, "Where did he go then?"

"He said he was going in to watch Ted examine poor Mr. Evans."

Henry nodded and stood up. "I think I'd better go too."

"You men are very busy all of a sudden," Miss Robb said acidly, "but don't think I'm going to do all these dishes alone, because I'm not."

"Let them rot," Henry retorted, and left the room.

He went out to the porch and into the other side of the house and then realized that he had forgotten his flashlight. It was very cold and very dark, but he could hear Gilling and Ted talking not far away.

"—don't seem to have any matches on me," Gilling was saying.

"Damned lighter never works when I need it most," Ted muttered.

Henry supposed that his opening the front door had blown out their candle and began to fumble in his pockets for matches, but could not find any. He heard Ted make some remark about having finished, anyway, and the two of them apparently decided to leave.

They passed close to Henry, and he said, "Wait for me," but they were still talking and didn't hear him. He found himself near the dining room, and he peered in and could see the shape of Scrimmer's head, with the hat still on it, outlined against the window. He thought of Claude, coming into this black, dusty room and talking to that dead face, with its sagging jaw and dim eyes, and shivered.

And then his heart seemed to plunge up into his throat as the dead man's head moved slowly around.

Chapter 24

HENRY DREW his breath in sharply, and the head moved back again. He took a step into the room and felt for the gun. It was gone. He hadn't even a flashlight, and he stood for a moment, looking at the still figure and listening to the thumping of his own heart, and then he backed out again and went swiftly along the hall to the front door. He was more accustomed to the darkness now and was able to make his way without fumbling. The door stuck a little, but he gave it a frenzied pull, and it swung inward.

The front porch glittered in the cold, brilliant moonlight, but Henry turned his back on it and went in at the other door. In the dining room Gilling and Diana were standing in front of Claude, who lay back in his armchair, sipping wine.

"Gilling," Henry said abruptly, "I want you to come into the other side with me. There's something—"

Claude came plunging out of his chair, brandishing the gun that Henry had so recently missed. He cried wildly, "I'll kill them—all those crooks—rats—I'll kill them. There's no hope for anyone, not until the day"—he paused, and looked around at the three shocked faces rather blankly—"the day that never comes." He paused again, and then raised the gun and waved it around. "I'll shoot them all. I'll get rid of them—"

Diana caught his arm and clung to it, pleading, "Papa, don't. Just forget about it, darling. Please!"

Gilling and Henry moved in quietly and quickly, and Gilling took the gun, which was now dangling limply in Claude's hand. Henry immediately took it from Gilling with the brief explanation, "You have one already, and I don't."

Diana was saying gently, "We'll go to bed, Papa. We're all tired. Come on, dear. We'll help you."

"Best thing to do," Gilling agreed. "Someone get him a cup of coffee. It—it will calm him down."

"I'll get it," Diana said quickly. "You go up to bed, Papa. They'll help you, and I'll bring you a nice cup of coffee."

Claude looked around at them and then irritably freed himself from Henry and Gilling, muttering, "Let go of me."

But he went upstairs quietly enough and allowed them to undress him and put him to bed. Diana presently appeared with a cup of steaming coffee, but as she approached Claude, Gilling stepped forward and took it out of her hands. "Too hot," he said briefly. "I'll cool it off a little."

He went out into the hall, and Henry followed him, while Diana sat down by the bed and began to stroke Claude's forehead. Henry watched with interest while Gilling dropped a powder into the coffee and presently asked, with reluctant admiration, "Do you always carry stuff like that around with you? You know, sometimes I wish I'd been a detective. I think I'd have been good."

Gilling, who had supposed himself unobserved, frowned in annoyance and disdained to reply. He took the coffee to Claude, who drank it down in three gulps and said gratefully, "Thank you, baby, that was what I needed. I'm sorry I sounded off like that, but I've had a shock."

"What was the shock?" Gilling asked, but Diana shook her head at him. "Not now. Papa must go to sleep, and I'll stay with him until he does. You two go away and leave us. Right now."

Henry led Gilling into Diana's room, where a single candle flickered on the bureau. "We can wait here until he goes to sleep, and then we'll have to go into the other side of the house. I want you to see that moving corpse."

Gilling sat down and took out a cigarette. He gave Henry a rather chilly glance and said flatly, "So the corpse is moving now. No wonder the old buster in there is shaping up for a straitjacket."

"Oh, shut up and listen to me, will you?" Henry said impatiently. He told of his experience and ended up on a faintly defensive note. "I had no flashlight and no gun, so I thought I'd better come back here and equip myself before I started anything. And then Claude began to stick straws in his hair, so I haven't been able to get back."

"You are bearing up admirably," Gilling said, blinking at him through cigarette smoke. "As for the corpse, don't be too sure that it moved. That's one of the easiest things to be fooled on. Dim light. Your own state of nerves. You'd be surprised. We'll go in and have a look, but you'll find that he's still there and still dead."

"O.K.," Henry said, trying to appear cool and indifferent and finding himself furiously annoyed instead. "You know best, of course, always. But I *know* the thing moved, and we'd better go in there."

Gilling got up restlessly and peered into the other room. He muttered softly, "Damn it, he's still awake. He should be out by now. We can't leave the girl alone with him until he's well away. It'll need the two of us if he gets violent." He lighted a second cigarette on the stub of the first and added abstractedly, "I wonder where that damned doctor is. He could be watching him now."

"Perhaps he saw the corpse move, too," Henry said coldly. "And where is Mrs. Evans? I thought she was in this room."

Gilling looked at his cigarette as though he wondered where it had come from, and absently disposed of it in the hair receiver on the bureau. He produced a toothpick and muttered as he chewed on it. "Nah, that Robb number made up two beds in the room up the hall."

"But that's my room."

"Not tonight, son," said Gilling. "Listen, let's you and I get a few things straight."

Getting the few things straight developed into Gilling giving Henry an extensive grilling. He asked so many questions, and so many of them two and three times, that Henry lost patience entirely.

"Well," Gilling said after a while, "I'm getting somewhere, I think."

"So you are," Henry said furiously. "You're getting right back to the beginning of the circle where you started."

"I'll lay it out for you," Gilling replied composedly, "and you can correct me if you think I'm mistaken."

"How would the wrong end of a horse like myself know when anybody was mistaken?"

"You got to your office an hour too early, by error, and ran into Scrimmer, who had come to see Mr. Boster, probably by appointment over the phone. Boster was prepared to help Scrimmer complete his escape, perhaps with ready cash. Or it might be that Scrimmer had cash and was going to hand some over to Boster in return for his cooperation. You were there, and they decided to use you to make the police believe that Scrimmer was still in town."

"You mean they cooked up the story about Scrimmer trying to get revenge by shooting at Diana?"

Gilling nodded. "So Boster sent Scrimmer out here with Evans. Why here, I wonder?"

"I didn't think you ever had to wonder about anything," said Henry, who was playing with the soft wax at the top of the candle.

Gilling shrugged. "They had no keys, but a man like Scrimmer can always get along without keys, and I suppose they figured that it was a pretty good hideout. Evans was needed to get Scrimmer out here, and you were bribed to hang around and protect the girl. A couple of shots were fired so that the dumb cops would think the man was still in town."

"I was not bribed," said Henry stiffly. He made two little balls out of the wax and laid them side by side on the bureau. "Anyway, what sort of a crooked deal did Claude have with Scrimmer? Did you say Scrimmer owed him money?"

Gilling accidentally broke his toothpick, and fired the two halves at the wastebasket. He produced a fresh one, and said thoughtfully, "I assume the man owed Boster money. He must have. I know that Boster needs money right now—he's in debt—and I know that he made a lot of promises to pay up at the end of the month. It seems likely that he expected some from Scrimmer, since he went to such trouble to help him, hiding him under his desk when he called in Miss Robb and then shipping him out here, and even firing a couple of shots over your head to keep the police interested."

Henry went to the door of the other room and listened, but Claude seemed to be as wide awake as ever. He was telling Diana about when he was a little boy and went fishing.

Gilling went on, "The shots actually backfired on him, because they scared you into a panic, and you came running out here."

"I came out here for a few days of rest after leaving the hospital," Henry said distinctly, "and never ran once."

He heard voices on the stairs and moved to the door to see who it was. Miss Robb and Ted came up, and Henry asked, "Where have you two been?"

"We were cleaning up that hideous mess in the kitchen," Miss Robb said crossly, "and I'm not going to do it again."

"I thought you weren't going to do it even once."

She shrugged. "Early childhood impressions. I hate mess."

"Hear all the excitement a few minutes ago?" Gilling asked, his eyes moving over their two faces.

"We heard old chubby yelling," Ted admitted, "but with him it could be a hair in his soup or a mortal wound, so we stuck to the dishes. Baby came out to get him some coffee after a while and said he wasn't well. Maybe I ought to look at him, at that."

"Don't shake him up much," Gilling said. "I gave him something, and he ought to sleep now. He seems to have had some sort of a brainstorm."

Ted murmured, "Ah?" and Gilling added, "Just go in there and sit with him and the girl, will you? Keep an eye on him."

Ted nodded and walked briskly through into the other room, and Miss Robb bestowed a provocative little smile on Henry. "You see now how nicely it will work out for you to be my boyfriend?"

"Robby," he said in an exasperated voice, "will you kindly stop it?"

"Oh well," She sighed. "It's so lousy boring out here that I have to do something."

"Get Ted to play with you."

She shook her head. "He's too easy. It was like taking candy from a child to make him do the dishes. Listen, what's the matter with the boss? That yelling sounded a bit different to me."

Henry raised a shoulder and dropped it, and Gilling said smoothly, "Don't you think you should go in and see to Mrs. Evans, young lady?"

"No," said Miss Robb shortly. "If you think she needs seeing to, you'd better do it yourself."

Gilling said, "Hmm."

"That's telling him," Henry said admiringly.

"No, it isn't," Miss Robb snapped. "No one needs to tell him anything. He knows it all already. He just has to be reminded from time to time."

"We're going into the other side," Gilling said equably. "Would you care to come?"

She shivered and said hastily, "No indeed. Does my boyfriend have to go with you?"

"Yes, I do," Henry declared firmly.

Diana's voice said from behind them, "Don't be churlish, Henry, stay with your girl."

He turned slowly and said, "No, I'm trying to cast her aside like an old shoe."

Miss Robb giggled, and Diana murmured a bit abstractedly, "I think that's what is known as being a cad."

Gilling made an annoyed sound by manipulating his tongue against the roof of his mouth and moved off, and Henry followed him, refusing to admit to himself that Diana and Miss Robb together were too much for him.

Downstairs, Henry picked up his flashlight, and he and Gilling went out and into the other side. They walked quietly down the hall together and hesitated, without words, at the entrance to the dining room. Their two flashlights snapped on and the beams streamed across the room and highlighted the chair on which Scrimmer had rested for so long.

The chair was empty.

Chapter 25

GILLING SWORE quietly, and Henry, with his flashlight still playing on the empty chair, muttered, "The man was dead. He was dead. The body must be around somewhere. Someone's moved it."

Gilling swung his flashlight slowly around the room. "You can't be absolutely sure of that. You're not a doctor."

"He had a hole in his head," Henry said patiently, "a bullet hole. He was also cold and stiff. But of course the hole might have been merely for ventilation, and perhaps if we'd put him in a slow oven the stiffness might have disappeared. As you say, I'm not a doctor."

"O.K.," Gilling murmured, "keep your shirt on. We'd better have a look around."

The body was not in the dining room, nor was it in the kitchen. They came back through the hall to the front of the house and went into the living room, where Evans still lay in chilly immobility, but Scrimmer was not there.

When they had finished searching, Gilling walked over and looked down at Evans.

"Looks like a heart attack all right."

"You got your M.D. by just mailing the coupon and sending no money, for ten days' free trial?" Henry asked politely.

Gilling shrugged. "Not exactly. The young man with the doctor's diploma said it was a heart attack."

"Do you think he knows what he's talking about?"

Gilling yawned. "I'm tired, and I need sleep. This will hold for a while. Boster seems to have gone off his turnip. Maybe he's moving bodies around."

"No, he hasn't had the opportunity, not since I saw someone in that chair moving."

Gilling turned abruptly and went out, and Henry followed him back into the other house. The candle still burned at the foot of the stairs, and Henry blew it out as they went up.

Ted met them at the door of Diana's room. He asked, "Where have you been all this time? Old chubby is in a restless sleep, but he looks all right to me."

"Naturally," Henry agreed. "They have to be dead for at least a couple of hours before it dawns on you that something is wrong with them."

"Yeah," Ted agreed, "and they have to be treading the corridor to the electric chair before it dawns on you that they might need a lawyer. Listen, shut up, will you? Where can I sleep? I have to be off early tomorrow."

"Where are you going, son?" Gilling asked.

"Back to my patients, for God's sake. Do you think their ills are suspended in space while I'm away?"

"A little vacation from your ministrations," Henry observed, "ought to start them well on the way to recovery. By the way, do they all sag forward—"

"All right, boys," Gilling said firmly. He turned to Henry and added, "Tell him where to sleep, son."

"I don't give a damn where he sleeps," Henry declared. "There are sheets, of a sort, in the linen closet."

Ted looked stricken. "You mean there isn't a bed made up for me?"

"Not that I know of," Henry said airily.

Ted departed in a fury for the bathroom and presently reappeared with some sheets under his arm. He went straight to the small sewing room, which Henry was pleased to remember contained a sagging couch with broken springs.

Diana appeared at the door to Claude's room and whispered urgently, "What is it? What did you find?"

"Scrimmer's gone," Henry said flatly.

"But he couldn't. He's dead. What do you mean?"

Claude appeared behind her in a vast expanse of purple-striped pajamas. He muttered, "Scrimmer. Scrimmer. He wasn't dead, and I knew he wasn't. I talked to him. I told him he was hurt and he cursed out Evans. He said Evans shot him, but he got better. He could walk around. He walked around. And we all thought he was dead. He did a good job of pretending to be dead. Only, you caught him—now, I mean—and I was worried about Diana. We came here, and there he was. I thought he was dead but of course he wasn't. He came and tapped me on the back."

Claude shuddered, and Gilling moved closer to him. "It's all right, Mr. Boster, nothing to worry about. You come on back to bed and get some sleep." He took him by the arm and led him into the other room, and Diana followed. When Claude had been put to bed, she drew the covers up under his chin and kissed him. "You must go to sleep again, Papa. You're very tired. In the morning everything will be all right. We'll be able to leave here and go back to the city."

Claude closed his eyes, and Gilling herded Diana and Henry into the other room. "I'm going to sleep in with him tonight. You two can sleep in here."

"What on earth are you talking about?" Diana asked indignantly. "Henry can't sleep with me."

Gilling closed his eyes for a moment and sighed. He opened them to say reasonably, "I never expected him to sleep with you. But he can use that couch over in the corner."

"That isn't a couch," Henry said, looking at it. "It's a chaise longue. I'd have to sleep with my head and shoulders sticking up in the air."

"You can put a chair at the end of it."

"I don't care whether he puts a chair at the end or not," Diana broke in hotly. "He can't sleep there. It—it's outrageous! Why can't he go into one of the other rooms?"

Gilling said "No," and his eyes had a cold glint. "This is the safest plan, and we're going to stick to it." He gestured toward the other room. "You can't tell about cases like that, and I might need help with him. I want another man close by. I need you, too, young lady, because you're the one who seems able to keep him quiet. Look on it as an emergency measure and kindly do as I say."

Diana threw Henry a helpless glance, and Henry cleared his throat and peered down at the toes of his shoes.

"Now," Gilling said briskly, "I'm used to waking at the slightest noise. We'll leave the connecting door open slightly, with a book in front of it, like this—"

He picked up a book from the bedside table, and Diana immediately snatched it out of his hand. "That's the book I'm reading, and I'm going to need it tonight. Anyway, I don't see why Henry can't go in and sleep with you and Papa."

"No," Gilling said patiently. "I don't want Boster to see two men guarding him. That alone might be enough to excite him. Now, suppose we all go to bed. I'm exhausted. Keep the door to the hall locked to make sure that Boster stays in these two rooms, and when you've finished reading, put the book on the floor in front of the connecting door here, leaving it partly open. That way, if he gets up without waking me, it's likely that he'll wake one of you. Now, hold the fort while I go to the bathroom."

He went out into the hall, and Henry removed his coat and peered, grinning, into the mirror of the bureau. "Would you mind looking the other way while I get into my nightshirt?" he asked courteously.

She gave him a furious glare. "I'll do nothing of the sort. I intend to stand here and stare at your knobby knock knees and caved-in chest."

Henry, who had been proud of his figure since early youth, was annoyed in spite of himself. He proceeded to remove his trousers and shirt in a temper, and stood revealed in his shorts and undershirt, with his shoulders thrown back and his stomach held in. He glanced at Diana, but she had seated herself on the side of the bed and appeared to be buried in her book.

Gilling came back and unexpectedly revealed himself as a bit of a prude. He frowned and said, "Don't parade around like that, son, you ought to have more respect for the lady. Get undressed in the bathroom and wear your robe over your pajamas all night." He turned to Diana and added, "Remember, I'll be right in the next room. If he forgets himself, you can call me at any time."

Diana looked up and said briefly, "I'm not afraid of him."

Henry longed to devastate them both but could not assemble the right words. He went into the other room, got his pajamas and robe, flung them onto the chaise longue, and then stalked off to the bathroom in silence.

When he came back, he found Diana in bed, reading by the light of the single candle. She wore a tailored woolen robe of navy blue, and her hair lay in flaming magnificence on her shoulders. Henry made straight for his pajamas and robe, which, in his confusion, he had forgotten to take to the bathroom. The robe was there, but the pajamas had disappeared, and after he had searched futilely for a while, Diana looked up at him.

"Gilling took your pajamas. He has nothing with him at all, and he figured you could wear your robe over your underclothes."

Henry started for the other room in a cold fury, and she said sharply, "For heaven's sake, don't start another fuss. Let the poor man sleep in peace. He's exhausted."

Henry stuck his head through the door and realized that Gilling was already snoring vociferously. Claude seemed quiet, and after a moment he backed away and went to the chaise longue. He sat with his shoulders propped up against the back, since any other arrangement necessitated dangling his legs over the end, and lighted a cigarette in dignified silence.

Diana glanced at him. "Don't make too much of a fog of smoke in here. We can't open the window."

"Why not?"

"Too cold. It's bitter outside, and these old houses—"

"These old houses," said Henry, "have plenty of cracks for the smoke to get out."

"I wish I could get out as easily as the smoke."

"Do you?" Henry looked at her. "What time this morning did Miss Robb and Mrs. Evans get here?"

"I don't know." She wrinkled her forehead. "I've thought about it, and I've come to the conclusion that it was as early as when we were drinking coffee in the kitchen, which is why we didn't hear them. Mrs. Evans was exhausted, and so Miss Robb took her right upstairs—she had to go to the bathroom first—and then Miss Robb put her right down on my bed and didn't bother to take anything off her except her shoes. It seems they didn't know the storm was so bad, or they'd never have come, but Miss Robb knew somebody was here because the house was warm. Of course she knew her way around inside, since she must have been out here many times—naturally."

"Why 'naturally'?" Henry asked stiffly. "As a matter of fact—"

"Oh, skip it." Diana shook vivid hair back from her face impatiently. "Miss Robb said she had quite a time with Mrs. Evans. Her fingers and toes had gone numb, and she had to rub them until the circulation began to come back, and then Mrs. Evans said the tingling was so bad she could hardly stand it. By the way, what's her first name?"

"Mrs. Evans? She's never confided in me to that extent."

"Idiot. I mean Miss Robb."

"I do not know Miss Robb's first name," Henry said carefully.

"That sounds like a stupid lie to me, and I cannot for the life of me see why you bother to tell it."

Henry drew in breath for a devastating reply, but someone knocked on the door, and he walked over to answer it in haughty silence instead.

Ted stood outside, and he said rather formally, "It has occurred to me that I forgot to tell you or the hairless policeman that Mr. Evans died some hours before that Scrimmer fellow."

Chapter 26

HENRY SAID, "Oh, then Evans could not have killed him, unless you are making a mistake."

"I do not make mistakes of that kind," Ted said coldly. "I'm sorry it doesn't happen to suit you this way, but there it is. Now, how does it happen that you have such a nice room to sleep in, when a guest like myself is pushed off into the outer darkness?"

He walked into the bedroom and stopped short at the sight of Diana comfortably propped up in bed, with a book in her hands and her hair floating luxuriantly around her shoulders.

"Baby!" he yelled reproachfully. "I would never have thought it of you. And with a crumb like Debbon too."

"Will you shut up!" Henry whispered fiercely. "You know about Boster's condition. He's right in the next room. I'm here in a protective capacity."

"Undressed? In your robe?"

"Pick your mind out of the gutter. I'm in my robe so that I can relax on the chaise longue over there. I happen to know that you have a better bed than that. Gilling is in the next room, too, with the door open, as you can see."

Diana had lowered the book onto her lap and was looking exasperated. "For heavens' sake, will you stop calling me 'Baby'? My name is Diana."

"Certainly," Ted said stiffly. "No offense intended, I'm sure."

He backed out into the hall, and Henry followed him. "I should think," Ted whispered immediately, "that she'd be decidedly uncomfortable with you in there."

"What do you mean? Why should I make her uncomfortable?"

"Well"—Ted shrugged—"Miss Robb might come in and find you together, and wouldn't that be something to dream about after a lobster supper?"

"Will you, for God's sake, go to bed?" Henry asked patiently. "Miss Robb is no doubt sound asleep, and even if she found me bedding down in a dormitory at Vassar, it would be no concern of hers."

Ted gave a nasty laugh. "You think not? Is that the joint where the sweet young things make a daisy chain every spring? She'd wind it around all their necks and strangle them one by one."

"Are you trying to wake her up so that she can join the fray?" Henry asked ominously.

"Mrs. Evans is snoring under a sedative," Ted said, "and will be snoring under it all night, which means that Miss Robb has little chance of getting to sleep in the same room. In fact, I doubt whether I'll be able to get to sleep as far away as my room. Anyway, it's a question whether Miss Robb is even in bed. Who knows where that one is at any time?"

"I don't give a damn where she is," Henry said, in complete exasperation. "Go on back to your room. You might find her there."

He retreated into the bedroom and closed and locked the door. Diana had put her book away, and she said, "Get to your chaise, and shove a chair onto the end of it. I'm blowing out the candle, and I'm going to try to get some sleep."

Henry pulled a chair over to the end of the chaise and said dispiritedly, "I know it won't be comfortable, but it will be something to hang my feet on."

Diana blew out the candle and said into the darkness, "If I don't leave here tomorrow, I'll get that Ted man to examine my head." She has forgotten about putting the book in front of the door, and it lay on the floor beside her bed.

Henry made no answer, because he was thoroughly uncomfortable. He knew that he could never sleep in such discomfort and with so many puzzling things running through his head. It would be impossible. He'd certainly be awake all night. His eyes closed, and he began to snore gently.

In the other room Claude awoke suddenly and broke into a nervous perspiration when he realized that he had been asleep. He listened with straining ears, heard Henry's snores, and braced himself. Diana did not snore, and there was no way of knowing whether she was asleep, but he'd have to chance it. He'd be quiet, so quiet that perhaps she wouldn't hear him, even if she were awake.

The bed creaked as he got out of it, and Gilling stopped snoring. He froze where he was, and after a while Gilling began to snore again. Claude headed for the next room, step by cautious step. If Diana were awake and caught him, then he'd just have to pretend that he was going to the bathroom. He was barely breathing, and his feet were cold. If he got as far as the hall downstairs, he'd get something out of that hat rack to put on his feet. He stepped on a small, hard object, and froze again as pain shot through his foot. He must not lose his head now. He was almost out. And he *had* to make it.

The door was dangerously close to the head of Diana's bed. He put cautious hands on the lock and then felt up and down for a bolt. There was a bolt, and it took him an uncomfortably long time to discover that it had not been shut. That fathead Henry, careless as usual, had probably left it open and the powder the lousy cop had given him made him dizzy and unsure of himself. But he had only to turn the lock—and these old locks were usually loose, and turned easily.

It turned easily, but it made a slight scraping noise. Diana moved, and Henry stopped snoring. Claude held his breath and stood perfectly still, mentally cursing Henry first and then deciding that he should never have tried it. He should simply have let the drug have its way and gone to sleep. Only, what was the use of thinking that way? He had to see to it. Maybe it was all done by now. Maybe it was over with, but he couldn't really believe it. He had to know. Maybe, for once— No use hoping, though.

He realized that Diana was lying still and Henry was snoring again, and Gilling was trumpeting from the other room too. This was the hardest part, opening the door. It was bound to creak. There wasn't a door in the whole blasted sagging house that opened quietly.

He stood in sweating indecision for a while and then decided to risk everything by opening the door with one swift pull during one of Gilling's snores. Perhaps Henry would contribute at the same time, and that should drown out the noise of the door. He realized suddenly that Gilling had stopped snoring, and he held his breath again through a moment of agony. His hand was damp on the doorknob, and he was about to dry it on his pajamas when Gilling started to snore again, and without waiting to think Claude gave the door a sharp pull. It opened without making any noise whatever.

He stepped outside and pulled the door behind him but did not close it, since he had to get back in again. Not that that was too important, of course, since he could always say that he'd just been to the bathroom if anyone roused. Still, it would be better if no one knew that he had been out at all.

He crept down the stairs, his hand clinging to the banister as he tried not to stumble in the darkness. At the bottom he groped for the hat rack and fumbled through the confusing assortment of overshoes. He managed to find two rubbers and put them on his feet, although they were not mates. One flapped dispiritedly as he walked, and the other cramped his toes uncomfortably.

He groped his way through the dining room and the butler's pantry and around the kitchen table to the cellar stairs. He stood at the top, looking down into the darkness, and at last he called softly. There was no answer, and presently he went down, going slowly and heavily from step to step, his breath grunting in his throat. He went straight to the furnace. He opened the door and looked into a fire that was burning so fiercely that he drew back with a little shudder. He shut the door with a bang and hastily made his way back to the stairs. He climbed, puffing, to the kitchen and through to the front hall, where he stopped. Well, no help for it. He'd have to go in. Just go in, that's all. He pulled a coat from the hat rack and put it on over his pajamas. Both front doors opened a bit more easily now. Sloppy arrangement to have front doors that merely jammed without locking. Typical of the Debbons, though. Both Henry and his aunt would have made good interior decorators for any nuthouse. Oh well, mustn't think of that now. Mustn't get excited. All his trouble came from getting too excited.

He pushed through the door into the other house and made his way quietly to the dining room. There was a little moonlight on this side, and a cold white finger of light lay across Scrimmer's chair. It touched Scrimmer's slouch hat showing above the back of the chair, and Claude sagged against the doorjamb, and moaned, "Oh, my God!"

Chapter 27

THERE WAS A faint sound from the direction of the front door, and Claude held his breath. That damned sneaking busybody, Gilling—it must be. Only, perhaps it wasn't. Perhaps—Claude felt his legs go weak for a moment, and then he pulled himself together and plunged toward the chair.

Gilling stood just inside the front door. He knew that he must be absolutely quiet, that Claude must not hear him if he were to get an accurate check on the degree of the old buster's lunacy. Scrimmer's body had disappeared, and Claude maintained that he wasn't dead. And maybe he wasn't. But Claude had gone nuts just when they could have searched for Scrimmer, dead or alive. Or for someone else.

Gilling moved slowly down the hall without using his flashlight. With any luck he might be able to finish this job now and get some sleep. He edged into the dining room.

It seemed to be deserted. He circled around cautiously and discovered that Scrimmer's chair was vacant, with the rug that had covered him lying across the arm. He went on to the kitchen, going more quickly now and using his flashlight, but the room was empty.

He hesitated and then heard the unmistakable sound of the front door. He went swiftly through the hall and found it closed, and outside the moonlight lay cold and still on the blank expanse of snow.

He went into the other side and stood still in the hall, listening, but there was no sound. He hadn't been careful enough, that was all. Claude had heard him. And surely Claude must be sane, because he had evaded him deliberately, unless it was the cunning of lunacy. Gilling mounted the stairs and went into the communal bedroom of Diana and Henry. The candle was flickering on the bureau, and Henry sat on the side of the chaise longue smoking a cigarette.

"What's going on?" Gilling asked abruptly.

Henry shrugged and flicked ashes into the hair receiver. "Claude's been walking in his sleep."

"Who says so?"

"Diana. And Claude agrees with her."

Gilling yawned. "That's as good a story as any."

"You been walking in your sleep, too?" Henry asked.

"I might as well have been," Gilling muttered, and made for the other room.

He found Diana seated on the side of Claude's bed, stroking his forehead, and he stood looking down at them. Claude glared back balefully.

Diana glanced up. "I thought you were going to wake up if he so much as stirred."

"I did."

"Then what d'ya want to let me get all the way into the other side of the house for?" Claude demanded. "It was a very nasty shock."

"Go on back to bed, young lady," Gilling said composedly. "He'll be all right now, and I need some sleep."

Diana looked doubtfully at Claude, and he said, "Yes, baby, you go to bed. You look tired out. I'm all right, and we'll go home first thing in the morning."

"Aren't you afraid," Gilling asked, "with Scrimmer hanging around loose?"

"Ah, shut up !" Claude snarled, and added, "Go on, baby. Please."

Diana kissed him and went back to the other room, where Henry gave her an inquiring look. She said briefly, "Give me a cigarette."

He supplied her and pulled one out for himself. "It's only five o'clock," he said, throwing the match stub at the hair receiver and missing. "I thought it was almost morning."

"I know, but I don't care. I'm going to stay awake anyway. I can't take a chance on Papa getting up again. Besides, I don't believe I could sleep. I'm all upset." She got back into bed and arranged her pillow so that it supported her against the headboard.

Henry established himself on the chaise longue with his shoulders upright against the back. "I think I drowsed for a while. I can get along without any more sleep."

"Drowsed!" She stared at him. "You were sleeping like a hog. Snoring, too. I thought the plaster would fall."

"I never snore," he said stiffly. "That was Gilling."

"You were sleeping when Papa came back, and I woke up before Gilling came. It was you who were snoring, because Gilling wasn't here."

Henry exhaled smoke in offended silence, and Gilling appeared in the doorway.

"Is Papa asleep?" Diana asked.

Gilling nodded. "I don't think he wanted to, but the drug got him as soon as he lay down and pretended to be asleep."

"What do you mean, 'pretended'?" she asked indignantly.

"He's still pretending," Henry said, apparently addressing the ceiling.

Gilling shook his head. "No, he isn't. I suggest, young lady, that you go in and watch him while Mr. Debbon and I go out and pick up this mysterious person who seems to be hanging around."

Diana said, "No!" very firmly.

"But, my dear young lady, I can't waste any more time. I need sleep badly."

"The sort of snoring you do," Henry said sourly, "would exhaust anyone."

"I won't stay here alone," Diana declared shrilly.

Gilling compressed his lips. "Then you'd better get Miss Robb in to stay with you."

"Oh no, I don't want her." She turned to Henry. "You'd better get Ted to come in."

Henry said, "Well—" and Gilling broke in peremptorily. "Lock yourself in here with Mr. Boster, and you'll both be safe enough."

"But you know perfectly well that Papa is—isn't quite—"

"I believe he's as sane as I am," Gilling said coldly. "But in any case, he won't hurt you." He cleared his throat and turned to Henry. "Either you're coming with me or you're not. I should prefer you to come, since I'll need you to hold the flashlight. I want to have my gun ready, because I think that one of Scrimmer's pals is hanging around."

Diana gave Henry a narrow-eyed look. "If you go around holding a flashlight, you'll make a nice target for this pal of Scrimmer's."

"We shall be cautious, naturally," Gilling said. "Of course, if there is no pal of Scrimmer's around, then things look bad for Mr. Boster. It would whitewash him considerably if we could pick up someone."

Diana shivered and whispered, "Oh, go on. I'll stay here."

Henry felt very unwilling to leave her alone, but as he hesitated, Gilling whispered urgently, "Come on, will you! She's the only one who is safe."

Henry belted his robe tightly over his underwear and pulled the flashlight out of his pocket. He followed Gilling reluctantly down to the dining room and asked, "Aren't we going to the other house?"

"No. The old boy is trying to persuade us that Scrimmer is still alive, but he's covering up for the other one, whoever he is. He wants us to think that Scrimmer has been responsible for all the activity."

"But—"

"So of course they have to get rid of Scrimmer's body completely, probably by way of the furnace."

Henry nervously rebelted his robe and followed Gilling through to the kitchen.

Gilling listened for some time at the top of the cellar stairs and then instructed Henry to play his flashlight down the length of them. They went down slowly and cautiously, and Henry was conscious of the fact that his toes were curling in because he half expected to have them shot off.

There was no sound, and no one to be seen, and Gilling went straight to the furnace. He opened the door and stood looking at the great pile of glowing coal, and at the same time, Henry noticed that the blower was open. He closed it with a bang and muttered, "Somebody seems bound to burn up all the coal before morning."

Gilling nodded. "Naturally, they have to wait until the fire comes up a bit before putting him in. He's probably hidden around here somewhere. We'll have to search the cellar very thoroughly. Be careful and keep close to me."

Henry kept as close as was humanly possible, and they made an extensive search, but they did not find Scrimmer. Gilling was annoyed, and said irritably, "I could have sworn we'd find the body down here somewhere, all ready to go in."

Upstairs, Diana stopped her restless pacing and got back into bed. She lay smoking and trying nervously to identify the various noises that seemed to explode all over the house. Of course an old house was always full of queer noises, especially at night. It was all right when the others were with her, but with only Papa asleep in there—

Suddenly she was rigid, her breath arrested, and the smoke from her cigarette rising silently into the air.

There was a distinct sound of whispering from Claude's room.

Chapter 28

DIANA FOUND that her teeth were chattering, and she got out of bed and pulled a robe around her. Why should Papa be whispering in there? When he had nightmares, they were always shouting nightmares. She picked up the candle, which was guttering close to the end by now, and turned her eyes away from the shadows that leaped from her shaking hand. As she made her way to the connecting door, she realized that the whispering had stopped.

Claude was asleep. She looked at him closely and decided, uneasily, that he was not shamming. His eyes were closed, and the breath whistled slowly through his open mouth. She hesitated, wondering why her teeth were still chattering, and then noticed that the candle in here was much longer than her own. She exchanged them, blew out the stump she had been carrying, and returned to her own room. She put the fresh candle on the bureau and began silently to pace the room, because she was too nervous to go back to bed.

Downstairs, Gilling and Henry had come up to the kitchen, and Gilling went straight through to the hall and began to pull on an overcoat.

Henry raised his eyebrows. "Going for a walk? Mind posting a letter for me?"

"It stopped snowing some time ago," Gilling said patiently. "If anyone has left here, there will certainly be tracks to show which way he went."

Henry shrugged. "If anyone went, it wasn't Scrimmer. I tell you he was stiff and cold."

"Boster had someone with him when he was in here just now. I didn't see it, but I heard it and could not be mistaken."

Henry picked up an overcoat, and they went out onto the porch. There were no visible tracks, and after a moment Henry said, "If we want to be sure, we'll have to circle the house. He might have gone out across the back fields."

Gilling sighed and went back into the hall, where he began to pull on a pair of overshoes. Henry stamped into his own, and they presently made their way down the porch steps and swung around the side of the house. It was much easier going now. The wind had dropped and the night was clear and bright and cold. Henry went ahead, his breath steaming from his mouth and his hands jammed into his pockets. Once he turned around and saw Gilling plowing out into the tracks where they had found Evans, and he changed his direction and followed. "This is where we found—"

"Evans. Yes, I know. I wonder why he ran out here."

"Claude will tell you. He'll be happy to. His version is that Evans scared himself by killing Scrimmer and ran out here in a dither."

"Well"—Gilling turned away—"people do odd things, especially in a dither. Perhaps that's what happened."

"That would be impossible, according to Ted," Henry objected. "He said Evans died quite some time before Scrimmer."

Gilling stopped abruptly and turned. "Is that what he told you?"

"Yes."

"And I tried to pump it out of him, and all he would tell me is that he thought Evans had died of a heart attack."

Henry grinned. "He was just being difficult. He's trying to build up a reputation as a good doctor."

Gilling went on in silence. They completed the circuit of the house without finding any tracks except Gilling's own, which had been blown over and could be seen only faintly, and presently went back inside. Gilling, stamping and blowing on his fingers, said flatly, "No one has left this house recently." He sat down and began to pull off his overshoes. "So we shall find them inside."

"Them?"

"Scrimmer, still dead, and somebody who's hand in glove with Boster."

Henry, blowing on his own numb fingers, asked vaguely, "Do you think this method really gets them warm?" and added, when he received no answer, "Who might be hand in glove with Boster?"

"Well, you, for instance."

"Me!"

"You or the redhead, or the old woman or that younger one who is so efficient that she'd never have let a sloppy thing like February 29 ball up the calendar if she'd had anything to do with it, or that brilliant young doctor pal of yours who probably doesn't know there is a February 29."

"You sound a little bitter," Henry said mildly. "Didn't you mention the possibility of one of Scrimmer's pals?"

"Any one of you might have been Scrimmer's pal. Boster certainly was." Gilling paused and cleared his throat. "Pals often kill each other, and then all the other pals get together and try to cover up. Right now, directly under my nose, they figure on putting Scrimmer in the furnace and dusting their hands off after a good job well done."

Henry thought it over. "But, look, it doesn't have to be one of us. Some closer friend of Scrimmer's could have joined him out here before the snow came. It seems likely, because some of our food was missing."

"Scrimmer could have taken the food. He was alive until some time this morning."

Henry nodded. "So Ted says, and I suppose he ought to know. He spent many years at his books—when he was sober, anyway."

"I'm going to make some coffee," Gilling said, yawning. "Something to keep me awake. You go up and see if everyone is asleep in his own bed as he should be and then come back. I'll have to find Scrimmer's body."

"How the devil am I supposed to find out whether they're in their own beds or not?"

"You ought to be able to solve minor problems of that sort," Gilling said, yawning again. "Open their doors and look in."

Henry went to the stairs and ascended quietly. In certain ways Gilling's presence was a comfort to him, and yet he had a childish desire to annihilate him completely.

He went straight to Ted's room, opened the door, and peered in. There was a faint light from the window, but it was not enough, and he had to use his flashlight. Ted was asleep, but he stirred restlessly, and Henry snapped off the flash and backed out. He found himself unreasonably irritated because Ted appeared to be one of those quietly superior sleepers who do not snore.

He went on to the room shared by Mrs. Evans and Miss Robb. He knew how to open this door quietly, but it would not have mattered, since the snores of Mrs. Evans were enough to drown out all minor sounds. He played the flashlight onto one of the beds, and Miss Robb sat up with a little cry.

"Hush," Henry said quietly, "I'm just checking up to see whether everyone's in bed."

"The perfect host." Miss Robb was a bit acid. "Are those the house rules? Everyone in his own bed?"

Henry backed out and went along to Diana's room, where he was taken aback to find the door locked. He tried it twice, and then Diana's voice spoke up from the other side.

"You two can find some other place to sleep. Papa and I want a little peace, so go away and leave us alone."

"Is he in bed?" Henry asked.

"It's none of your business. Kindly leave us alone until we can get out of this awful house."

Henry considered several replies and finally went off in offended silence. He returned to the kitchen, where he found that Gilling had made some breakfast to go with the coffee, and sat down to it with a sigh of pleasure.

They ate in silence for a while, and then Gilling said, "Scrimmer's body must be found. It's here somewhere. Now there's no use in making another futile search. You'll have to think it out."

Henry buttered a piece of toast and said callously, "Maybe they shoved him in the furnace."

"No. I looked. No traces."

"Well, there's something odd about the furnace, anyway. The dining room on the other side is cold, and it ought to be fairly warm by now. You see, the shutoff doesn't quite close, and the longer the furnace is on the warmer that side gets."

"Oh, that." But Gilling was silent for a moment, and then asked in a changed voice, "Hot air, isn't it?"

Henry, glancing around to make sure that they had eaten everything, nodded absently.

Gilling stood up. "Then the body is stuffed into the register."

Henry was annoyed at not having thought of it himself. He said repressively, "I very much doubt that it's large enough."

Gilling was already on his way out. It was still dark enough to make the flashlight necessary, but out on the porch there was the hint of a cold, still dawn. They went in at the other side and along to the dining room, where the musty air was still bleak and chilly. Gilling directed the flash onto the hot-air register, and they saw that it was open. Henry knelt down and removed the grating, and it was obvious at once that the pipe was clear of any obstruction but dust and cobwebs.

Henry smiled into Gilling's disappointed face and said, "You see? There wouldn't have been room to have pushed him in here, anyway."

Gilling turned away and muttered, "Then why is the room so cold?"

"I told you it was odd."

"Defective piping, perhaps. Probably always been cold."

Henry said, "No," and as Gilling started for the door, he added urgently, "Wait a minute."

"What is it?"

"There's a cold-air return in this room somewhere, and that *is* large enough for a body."

Gilling drew a long breath. "Where is it?"

It took them a few moments to find it, since it was under a light, high settee, and then they had some difficulty in removing the grate because Scrimmer's collar had become jammed under the edge. There was still more difficulty in pulling the body out, and Gilling, panting a little, muttered, "Must have been even harder to get him in. I don't see how they expected to convince us that Scrimmer was still alive."

"They?" Henry muttered. "What makes you think there's more than one? Boster could have killed him in a fury some time this morning."

"No. From what you say yourself, he didn't want him dead. There's something else. Evans running outside and dying of a heart attack. Scrimmer not knowing where he went, and probably not caring. And then the snow, and you people turning up. So he got some food."

"What was he waiting for?"

"Boster," Gilling said grimly. "Boster, with everything arranged for his getaway."

"But Claude was in town. He was not intending to come out here. He came only because I was corning."

Gilling shook his head. "Boster was occupied with planting a red herring for the police. You see, you had seen Scrimmer in there. He had to do something to keep in the clear, too. He couldn't exactly go around and buy tickets somewhere and not go himself. But he could eventually get out here, wave good-bye to Scrimmer, and of course collect his half of the money, which, I have no doubt, was hidden out here all along."

Henry wrinkled his forehead. "But in that case, Claude could have collected his half at any time."

"All these crooks have friends, and Scrimmer was no exception. If the money had been missing when Scrimmer turned up to collect it, Boster's life would not have been worth a thin dime."

"But Scrimmer is dead. Why should Claude have been so upset?"

"Well"—Gilling gave his head a little shake—"he could have been acting, or he'd already been to the hiding place and the stuff was gone. Scrimmer was dead, and Boster's pal—he must have a pal—some-one—"

"Why was Claude sitting in front of that corpse and talking to it?" Henry asked, hoping that his voice sounded calmer than he felt.

"Hysterical reaction. Cursing at him, even though he was dead." Gilling ran a thoughtful hand over his bald head. "Cursing at the body, because he couldn't find the money, that's all."

Henry said doubtfully, "But later on he told him he'd bring him some food, and also said he would have to tell him where the money was."

Gilling looked up, and his face changed. "You're beginning to interest me," he said in an odd voice. "Quite interesting. And shortly after that the corpse is no longer there, with Boster going balmy in the head first, so that we won't rush in there right away. And then, mind you, Boster says that Scrimmer is still alive. As I said, it's all very interesting."

"Very," Henry agreed. "Except that I don't know what it's all about."

"You couldn't be expected to know what it's all about."

"With my inferior type of head, you mean?"

Gilling sighed and turned away, and Henry followed him in silence. They went back to the other house and through to the kitchen, where Gilling sat down and appeared to lose himself in thought.

Henry watched him until the sound of dragging footsteps coming down the hall diverted him, and he got up and went to the door. It was Mrs. Evans, fully dressed, but with her face sagging into gray lines and hollows.

Henry asked inadequately, "How are you feeling?"

"I couldn't sleep a wink all night. I just tossed and turned. I thought I might as well get up as lie there staring at the walls."

Henry thought of her vociferous snores, but said kindly, "Will you have some coffee?"

"Thank you, Henry, that's good of you. But I think you ought to go upstairs. Your aunt is weeping bitterly up there."

Chapter 29

HENRY STARED at her, and Gilling looked up. "What's that?" he asked sharply. "Which one is his aunt?"

Henry had had only one aunt, and he supposed that the old lady must be referring to one of the others. But which one? Surely not Diana or Miss Robb.

He said stupidly, "Aunt?"

"Of course, dear, the one who lives here, you know. Remember, we came down here one Sunday when my niece was out from Bayhurst. She had her car, and we drove out this way. Your aunt was very nice. I asked her if I could do anything just now, but she shook her head and went up the attic stairs. I didn't see her last night, and I hope she doesn't think—I mean, all this trouble—dreadful for her."

Henry was already out in the hall, and Gilling, close behind him, asked, "Isn't your aunt dead?"

"Yes, but apparently Evans never mentioned it to his wife. They drove out here a couple of times while she was still alive."

"Where are you going?" Gilling asked.

"I'm going to hunt for somebody who looks enough like my aunt to fool Mrs. Evans."

They started up the stairs, and Gilling said, "She told us your aunt headed for the attic. We'd better go straight up there."

They went cautiously, without using their flashlights, but they could not find anyone in the attic, and the door to the other house appeared to be undisturbed.

"I knew she wouldn't be here," Gilling said presently. "By the way, did your aunt wear a wig?"

"Wig?" Henry repeated a little indignantly. "Of course not."

"Are you sure?"

Henry realized that he wasn't sure, actually. He hesitated, and then said weakly, "How would I know?"

Gilling nodded with a satisfied air, and Henry asked, "Do you think someone is parading around in my aunt's wig, supposing she had one?"

"Did you ever dispose of your aunt's things?"

Henry shook his head. "I never did, and it wouldn't surprise me if I never do. Too much of a job."

Gilling nodded again, pulled out a toothpick, and went downstairs without further words.

Henry stopped on the second floor and decided to look in the bedrooms again. He found that Ted was still sleeping quietly and that Diana's room was still locked, but Miss Robb was missing. He went on down to the kitchen to report to Gilling.

Gilling had not returned to the kitchen, but Miss Robb was there talking to Mrs. Evans, who appeared to be freshly upset. She turned to Henry and moaned. "Oh, there you are. I'm so sorry, but I didn't know. No one had ever told me. I'd have sent a wreath if only you had let me know. Did my poor husband know? Surely he would have told me."

"It doesn't matter," Henry said hastily. "I suppose he knew and forgot to tell you. But who was it you saw upstairs a little while ago that you thought was my aunt?"

"Oh, it *was* your aunt," Mrs. Evans declared firmly. "Poor soul, wandering forlornly around with all the trouble in her house."

"You saw a ghost?" Miss Robb asked, with a side glance for Henry.

Mrs. Evans looked pained. "My dear, we don't call liberated spirits 'ghosts.' " She closed her eyes and put a hand to her head. "I must try to get in touch with my poor husband, but not yet, of course. The funeral—"

She dissolved into tears, but Miss Robb stopped the outburst with her usual efficiency.

She said flatly, "There are no ghosts, or whatever it is you call them, so you couldn't have seen one."

Mrs. Evans dried her tears at once and embarked upon a long dissertation on disembodied spirits which she herself had seen and even spoken to. Miss Robb took the opportunity to start preparing some breakfast, and paused in her work to ask Henry, "Shall we eat breakfast together, dear?"

Henry said, "No," and Miss Robb sighed. Mrs. Evans, diverted, looked from one face to the other and asked, "You two thinking of getting married?"

" I don't want to say too much," Miss Robb murmured, turning the gas low under the coffee, "but it is a great tragedy. We love each other, but there are obstacles which simply cannot be overcome, and so I shall have to sit back and watch him marry someone else."

"But surely—" Mrs. Evans gave them each a doubtful glance and let it linger on Henry. She asked, rather severely, "Which church are you being married in?"

"Miss Robb is teasing you," he said shortly. "She never yet sat back for anybody. When she decides to get married, she'll run the guy up the aisle by the scruff of his neck."

"Men!" Mrs. Evans exclaimed and sighed vastly. She began to give Miss Robb some pointers out of her long years of experience.

Henry found his mind settling on Miss Robb with a certain amount of speculation. She must know a great deal about Claude's business, he thought. In fact she must know all about Scrimmer. She had been in Claude's office before Scrimmer left. So perhaps that was it. She had come out here with the idea of getting her cut. She didn't trust Claude, of course, and probably she had decided that she'd just pick up something for herself. Maybe she had it all. Perhaps she'd been here in time to have shot Scrimmer, and she could have picked up the entire amount, whatever it was. Claude didn't have it, and he was almost hysterical, even if he was only pretending on the insanity angle.

Diana, Claude, and Gilling walked into the kitchen, and something in their faces caused Henry to stiffen defensively.

Diana faced him and said clearly, "I'm sorry, Henry, but Papa has told me all about it, and I feel that I must protect the others here. It's my duty to explain to the detective that I think you are the one who shot that man and then took all the money belonging to Papa."

Chapter 30

HENRY, BEREFT of speech for the moment, received support from an unexpected quarter. Someone yelled, "That's a lie!" and Ted stalked into the room, using his elbows to clear a path for himself. He glared around at the assortment of faces and added fiercely, "The Debbons may be a bit dumb, but they've never done a dishonest thing in their lives!"

"There can always be a first time," Gilling suggested mildly.

Henry, still too shocked to defend himself, stared at Diana, who stared back at him. After twice swallowing air he turned slowly to look at Claude, but Claude hastily dropped his eyes to his feet, rattled change in his pockets, and appeared to be lost in judicial thought.

"Now look," Gilling said reasonably, "suppose the four of us go into the dining room and talk this over. Mr. Debbon will want to hear the story."

"He knows it already," Claude muttered and added loudly, "I want my breakfast."

Mrs. Evans got to her feet at once and sighed. "Of course, life must go on. I'll get you something, Mr. Boster."

"No, you won't!" Claude bellowed rudely. "I want a good breakfast this morning. I need it. Would you be good enough to move away from the stove, madam?"

"Nonsense," said Mrs. Evans comfortably. "I'm sure I know more about cooking than any mere man."

Ted had moved over beside Henry and appeared to be belligerently ready to defend the Debbon honor against all attack, and Miss Robb was regarding them with an odd expression on her composed face.

Gilling said peremptorily, "Mr. Boster, you will kindly postpone your breakfast until later. Bring a cup of coffee if there's any there. If not, you'll have to wait for that, too."

"Oh, dear!" Mrs. Evans rattled the percolator. "I'm afraid Miss Robb made just enough for us, and we've finished it. But I can have some fresh for you in a few minutes."

"I'm having my breakfast now!" Claude yelled.

Diana took his arm. "Now, darling, be reasonable. This is a serious thing. We must explain it all to Mr. Gilling, and Henry should be there to tell his side of it."

"If Henry tells his side of it," Claude muttered, "nobody else will have a chance to shove a word in."

"Come on, Papa, we must be fair about this, in case there's a mistake."

She urged him into the dining room, and Gilling and Henry followed. Ted tried to go, too, but was firmly held back by Gilling, who told him that he could go on sticking up for his pal later.

In the dining room they sat in a circle, and Gilling, after clearing his throat twice, asked, "Now, who's going to do the talking?"

Henry remained grimly silent, and Diana turned to Claude. "Darling, shall I tell it, or will you?"

Claude seemed to be intent on the toes of his shoes. He mumbled, "You tell it. If you go wrong, I'll correct you."

Diana nodded. "I'm going to admit right away that Papa did something he shouldn't have done—some legal work for this man Scrimmer—and when he sent him a bill, Scrimmer made a bargain with him. He said he couldn't trust his pals to hold his money for him, except one who was in jail, but if Papa would hide it, then when Scrimmer came out of jail, Papa would get several times the amount of his fee for having taken care of it."

"Shady," Gilling commented.

"Well, yes, of course, that's where Papa was so wrong to have had anything to do with it. The money was in Scrimmer's safe, which he kept in an old shack of his out in the country. He was afraid some of his friends might find it there, so he gave Papa the combination."

"Some of his friends, or the police," Gilling said coldly.

Diana assumed a little frown and said querulously, "I've told you Papa did wrong. We're not trying to hide it. Anyway, Papa got the money, and then he didn't know where to hide it, until he was out here one weekend after Henry's aunt died, and he hid it in the other house. He put it in a metal fireproof box and hid it in the closet under the stairs, in there, away at the back."

She paused to take a long breath and to give Henry a sober look. His face remained expressionless, and she went on, "Papa was shocked when Scrimmer got in touch with him and said he had escaped, but he agreed to let him come to the office early in the morning. Henry must have got wind of it, because he was there early that morning, too, and poor Papa was frantic. He was afraid his business would be ruined, and his only thought was to get rid of Scrimmer and the money just as quickly as possible. He had no idea that Henry knew anything, so he made up that story about protecting me and even pretended to shoot at us so that Scrimmer would have a chance to get his money and go away. He sent Evans out with Scrimmer and was supposed to come later himself with a car for him to use.

"When we did get out here, Papa couldn't find an opportunity to go into the other house, what with Henry hanging around, and then, when they went in together, Scrimmer was dead in that chair, and Evans had disappeared. Papa went back alone as soon as he could and discovered that the money was gone—all of it. He looked through Scrimmer's pockets, and it wasn't there, and so then it came to him. Henry had been on the porch when he'd first hidden that money, and Henry must have spied on him, and spied on him in the office, too, so that he knew all about it and he'd taken the money. When poor old Evans came out with Scrimmer, and they found it gone, Evans tried to run away and was scared into a heart attack. Then, of course, Henry found an opportunity to get into the other house. He had to, because he knew there'd be trouble from Scrimmer "

"Why?" Henry asked, interrupting for the first time. "It seems to me Claude would have been the one to expect trouble, not me."

"Papa and Scrimmer could easily have traced their loss to you. I mean, you were right in the office—this is your house—it would be simple."

"Finish your story," Gilling said briefly.

"Yes, of course, only there isn't much more. A short while ago Papa left his key ring lying around in the office, and he caught Henry fooling with it. He figured that Henry had been taking off the key to the metal box and then going out and helping himself to money when he needed it. And of course replacing the key when he had an opportunity."

"Quite a trick, that one," Henry commented, "since he always keeps his keys in his pants pocket with his hand closed around them, jingling them."

"Who moved Scrimmer's body from the chair to the cold air register in there?" Gilling asked.

Diana looked a bit confused, and Claude glanced up. "He did. Matter of fact, I'm sorry for him. I knew what he was doing, so I tried to help him along. He seemed to have gotten rid of the body, so I did my best to give you the impression that Scrimmer was still alive."

"Did you give Evans the key to the metal box when he escorted Scrimmer out here?" Gilling asked.

"No, I was to bring it out myself."

"I see. Then it was not that particular shock which killed Evans, since they could not have known that the money was gone."

Henry was thinking of Miss Robb. Her name could easily have been substituted for his in this entire recital. She'd have had to be pretty quick about shooting Scrimmer, but she could have done it. She'd been giving the impression that she had come out here to see Claude on business, and Claude had been angry with her for coming. It was odd that Claude would tell a tale to the police which made him so vulnerable, just to pin the murder of Scrimmer on Henry.

He wouldn't. It was something else. Henry stood up suddenly and interrupted Gilling in mid-sentence.

"About Evans—I think I know what frightened him out of the house. It was the ghost of my aunt."

Chapter 31

GILLING STOOD UP. "That so?" he murmured, eying Henry. "You *could* have done all these things, you know. Even when you led me to Scrimmer's body in the cold-air return, it could have been to pull the wool over my eyes."

"The wool's all up in your skull," Henry said bitterly. "Why should I bother to pull it down over your eyes? I think the story we've just heard is quite true, except for the fact that I am not the hero, as stated."

Gilling turned to Diana and Claude. "Will you two go out to the kitchen now and have breakfast?"

Diana stood up, but Claude settled back into his chair. "I want to listen to what he has to say."

Gilling said, "No," and Diana pulled at Claude's arm.

"Come on, Papa. You're going to feel a lot better now that you have it all off your chest. It's always best to admit your mistakes and face up to them, and now that you've done it, you won't be so tense and nervous any more."

She helped him to his feet and led him out to the kitchen, but he insisted on creeping back and putting an ear against the dining-room door. All he heard, however, was Gilling and Henry walking out to the hall, followed by the distant closing of the front door.

He straightened up, and realized that he was hungry and that that Evans woman was fooling around the stove, which sent him back to the kitchen in a hurry.

"The coffee is ready," Mrs. Evans said, looking up at him, "but I really don't know what we are going to do. There seems to be no more coal, and the fire's going out, and there isn't much food left. Of course we have the cold lamb—"

Claude said, "Excuse me, madam, but that stuff is more like an old boot than cold lamb."

He elbowed her away from the stove and cooked breakfast for Diana and himself over the embers. As they sat down to it, Ted asked, "Aren't you going to offer me some of that? I'm starving."

"I hope you starve to death," Claude said, pouring coffee. "And if Diana tries to offer you any of hers, I'll spit on it."

"There's the lamb—" Mrs. Evans murmured in a distressed voice.

Ted went sulkily to the ice chest and pulled out the platter of lamb. "It stinks in there," he said, slamming the door.

Claude gave the meat a withering glance and observed, "That stuff would stink anywhere."

Miss Robb, sitting at the table with a cigarette, explained placidly, "The electricity is off, and that's what always happens when a thing like that happens."

Ted began moodily to eat the lamb. He said to Diana, "I suppose that man Gilling has taken poor Henry away, but I'm telling you that I'll fight for him if it takes my last cent."

"How many cents do you have altogether?" Miss Robb asked.

Ted said he couldn't be sure, because it depended on how many of his patients paid their bills. "It's to be hoped, for Henry's sake, that they both do," Claude said and stood up. "I'm going to lie down, baby," he told Diana. "I'm tired, and I'll rest until we're ready to go."

She nodded at him. "All right, darling, try and get a nice sleep."

Claude went off. In the front hall he stopped to listen and then started slowly up the stairs. They'd gone to the other side, the two of them together, and what were they doing there? He went on to his room and dropped heavily onto the bed, where he lay with his eyes closed.

He was listening, though, with his ears strained. From time to time he thought he heard them in there, but he could not be certain. When at last he did actually hear them, he realized that they had come back from the other side and were in this side, apparently going from room to room. They came into his room after a while, and he deepened his breathing and let his mouth sag open a little. He didn't want to talk to them, and they might as well think he was asleep.

They didn't stay long. He heard them look in the closet, and one of them seemed to be at the door. He should have locked that door again. They might wonder why it was suddenly unlocked.

They went out and downstairs, and Claude felt his body relax into the bed.

On the first floor Gilling was saying, "Now where?"

Henry muttered, "I assure you that Claude doesn't love me, and he doesn't love Miss Robb, either—"

Diana passed them with her chin elevated and went upstairs without a word.

They stood looking after her, and Gilling said thoughtfully, "He loves her, though." He rubbed his bald head and added fretfully, "We've searched the place from end to end."

"I don't care," Henry declared stubbornly. "We'll simply have to search some more."

Diana came down again, and her green eyes were troubled. "We've got to get Papa home. He's not well at all. He—he's whispering in his sleep again."

There was a moment of absolute silence, and then Gilling and Henry moved together. They went past Diana and up the stairs, and while Gilling entered Claude's room by way of the hall door Henry went around and through Diana's room.

Claude still lay on the bed with his eyes closed, and Gilling wandered over to the closet and looked in rather aimlessly. Henry, standing still in the middle of the room, was looking at the studio couch on which Claude lay. The couch, he knew, could be separated into two beds and was separated now. The small cot, which could be rolled out from the main body of the couch, stood against another wall, and Henry walked over to examine it.

"Nobody could fit under there," Gilling said disgustedly.

"No." Henry turned his attention to the studio couch on which Claude was still determinedly sleeping. Two or three inches from the floor— impossible, surely. Or perhaps it wasn't impossible, with the cot gone, and a resulting gap at the back.

Henry said, "Come out of there, Fred, or I'll shoot right through your father and into you."

Chapter 32

THERE WAS A movement from beneath the couch which Claude instantly tried to cover up by turning over. He opened his eyes and muttered, "What is it? What is it?"

Gilling had a gun in his hand, and he slid the couch away from the wall, with Claude still lying on it.

Fred wore the old brown dress that Henry remembered as being so much a part of his aunt, but the wig had fallen off, and Fred's scared, pallid face appeared under his own hair.

Claude scrambled up from the couch. "Don't say anything, Fred," he commanded peremptorily. "Don't say anything at all." He turned to Gilling and added, "This poor boy, here, it's the first insanity we've ever had in the family. He needs institutional care."

Gilling shrugged. "I suppose that's your best bet. Anyway, come on, the house is getting cold, and there's no more food." He asked Henry, "Can you move the car?"

"I can try."

"O.K., see what you can do." He had Fred by the arm, and as they moved out into the hall, they came face to face with Diana.

She screamed, "Fred!"

"Don't worry, baby," Claude said in a sick voice.

Henry went off to wrestle with the car and was surprised to find that it was not as difficult as he had anticipated. It bumped slowly through the snow with its chains rattling. As he brought it around to the front, he saw that there was an assortment of people waiting on the porch. Gilling was there, still with a firm hand on Fred's arm, and Claude, Diana, Ted, and Miss Robb.

Gilling approached the car, leading Fred, and said to the others, "You'll all have to wait until I can send someone out to pick you up."

Diana and Miss Robb resigned themselves to this decision at once, Miss Robb with a shrug and Diana with a remark to the effect that someone would have to stay with Mrs. Evans, anyway.

Claude merely got into the car and sat there, and Ted let out a shout that resounded over the snow-covered fields. He fortified his position by yelling that he had two babies coming up and added that one of them was twins.

In the end Henry got out of the driver's seat and Ted slid under the wheel, remarking with satisfaction that you couldn't allow babies to shift for themselves. Gilling and Fred got into the back, and Claude remained slumped in the front beside Ted. He called out, "Baby, you can come, too, I'll move over," but Diana smiled at him and shook her head. As the car drove off, he looked back at her uneasily until she was out of his sight.

"Ted's all over the lawn," Henry said critically. "I hope he avoids that lily pond this time."

Diana glanced up at him. "I'm sorry I, well, accused you. I believed that story Papa told me."

"Always keep a doubt in your mind when these men tell you a story," Miss Robb advised and urged Diana back into the house with a hand on her arm. "There's some of that lousy wine left. Let's drink it up."

Henry followed them to the dining room and asked, "Where's Mrs. Evans?"

Miss Robb was pouring wine. "She's in there with her late husband. You'd better leave her alone. She says she wants to tell him some things."

Henry nodded, and Miss Robb asked presently, "Who got the idea that Fred was hanging around here?"

"I did," Henry said promptly. "I knew that Diana's story sounded plausible, if you got someone else to play my part. I thought perhaps you—"

"Brilliant!" Miss Robb murmured. "And I thought you loved me!"

"When I thought of someone dressing up as my aunt," Henry continued, "Fred came to my mind right away. It's the sort of thing he'd do, but it didn't seem to be like you, somehow. The most important thing, of course, was the way Claude was trying so desperately to cover up and then getting himself thoroughly involved in order to pin the thing on me. He wouldn't do that for anyone but Fred."

"And for baby here," Miss Robb said, jerking an elbow at Diana.

Diana tossed her cloud of shimmering hair and took a sip of wine.

Henry nodded. "Yes. But it had to be someone who'd been out here ahead of us, someone who frightened Evans out of the house. I suppose the same effort was made to frighten Scrimmer, but he wouldn't scare. So he had to be shot."

"Fred's tactics," Miss Robb agreed laconically. "How did he know about your aunt's clothes?"

"He'd been out here. I suppose he came across them and thought it would be a good joke to scare somebody into a fit, and then remembered about it when he was desperate."

Miss Robb frowned and said, "I'm still a bit confused."

"Well, Claude slipped into the other house shortly after we arrived, while Diana and I were doing the dishes. Fred must have met him at the door and told him that the money was gone, and Scrimmer was waiting impatiently, and I suppose Claude had to go back and try to figure out what to do. In the morning he and I went in and found Scrimmer there dead. He knew that Fred had done it. He pulled himself together and tried to fix things up. He told Fred to put the body in the furnace. The fire was boosted to a terrific heat. But Fred stuffed the body down the cold-air return instead, and then he took off the wig and put on Scrimmer's slouch hat, and the robe to cover his skirt, and sat there pretending to be Scrimmer. This was after Ted had examined the body, and I suppose Fred figured it would be a good hiding place for him. No one was apt to come looking at him again, especially with the lights out."

"Why didn't he put the body into the furnace?"

"Well"—Henry shrugged—"you know Fred. He couldn't get around to it. He was scared of being caught on the way. Maybe he even took a nap. When Claude got down, after we were all asleep, he found him still there, with nothing done. Gilling chased them all the way back and up to the bedroom. Claude must have told Fred to run and get under the studio couch and pull it back to the wall over him, and then Claude made a rumpus and declared he had been sleepwalking when he woke us up with his noise."

"Us?" Miss Robb murmured, raising her eyebrows.

Henry cleared his throat and gazed at the ceiling, but Diana said firmly, "Henry and I slept in the same room last night."

Miss Robb moaned, "Oh, God! Why didn't Fred shoot me, instead of Scrimmer!"

"Shut up! Both of you!" Henry said loudly.

Miss Robb sighed. "Well, why did Fred go out into the hall and show himself to Mrs. Evans?"

"It was early morning, and no doubt Claude had told him to go out over the snow and get away. After all, no one had seen him, but of course Fred muffed it again. He ran into Mrs. Evans and knew that she would mention it, so he got back into his hiding place under Claude."

Miss Robb said, "So Fred took all the money?"

"Evidently. He'd had a key made, but Scrimmer didn't know that—he was waiting for Claude to show up. Fred knew he had to stop a meeting between Claude and Scrimmer, because if Claude opened that box in front of Scrimmer and found it empty, he was as good as dead. Fred must have confessed in a hurried whisper, and then, later, he couldn't stall Scrimmer any longer, so he shot him."

"Who used Fred's steamer ticket?" Miss Robb asked wistfully.

Henry shrugged, and Diana asked, "Did Fred give me that dope at the hospital?"

Henry did not answer at once, since he felt that he was not speaking to Diana, but the urge to show off as a great detective finally prompted him to inform the ceiling. "Of course. He couldn't get Claude alone, and he kept himself hidden in the next room and unlocked the bathroom door whenever he could. He never got a chance to face Claude and make a clean breast of it, so at last he left and came out here, where he went on with his silly nonsense. Claude knew that he was in there—and Scrimmer, too—so he urged me to search the place, hoping that we'd run across Scrimmer and shoot. Naturally, he was very much upset when we found Scrimmer already dead, shot from behind by Fred."

There was a short silence, and then Miss Robb announced that it was getting very cold.

"I suppose the fire's out," Henry said. "There's no more coal."

"Couldn't we put on some sticks of wood or something?" Diana asked.

Henry made no reply, and Miss Robb said, "Can't you even give her a civil answer?"

"No. I don't think I like her much."

Diana finished her wine and gazed into the bottom of the glass.

Miss Robb got to her feet. "I'll go in and see whether Mrs. Evans has got in touch with the spirit of Mr. Evans, so that you can sit here and dislike her without interference."

"Thanks," Henry said stiffly.

Miss Robb departed, and Diana stood up. Henry remained where he was and averted his eyes.

Diana said, "I think I know why Papa wanted to send Fred off on that boat. He sort of knew that Fred might get into trouble. He always did get into trouble. Poor Papa!"

"Oh yes, poor Papa!" Henry said bitterly. He kept his eyes away from her, but he heard her walking restlessly about the room. After a while she came back and settled down close to him. She was quite still for a few minutes, and then she said, "What sports are you interested in?"

Henry was astounded at the feeling of pleasure that seeped through his body. She had read those columns after all, and now she was seeking to be an interesting companion for him. He gave a gloating little smile.

Diana flounced away from him. "Oh, stay mad forever, if you want to," she said petulantly.

Henry got up and held her with an arm around her waist.

"Please! Be reasonable! Ask me some more things. Like am I interested in art, or music, or red hair."

THE END

About The Rue Morgue Press

The Rue Morgue vintage mystery line is designed to bring back into print those books that were favorites of readers between the turn of the century and the 1960s. The editors welcome suggests for reprints. To receive our catalog or make suggestions, write The Rue Morgue Press, P.O. Box 4119, Boulder, Colorado (1-800-699-6214).

Catalog of Rue Morgue Press titles as of June 2004

Titles are listed by author. All books are quality trade paperbacks measuring 6 by 9 inches, usually with full-color covers and printed on paper designed not to yellow or deteriorate. These are permanent books.

Joanna Cannan. This English writer's books are among our most popular titles. Modern reviewers have compared them favorably with the best books of the Golden Age of detective fiction. "Worthy of being discussed in the same breath with an Agatha Christie or a Josephine Tey."—Sally Fellows, *Mystery News*. Set in the late 1930s in a village that was a fictionalized version of Oxfordshire, both titles feature young Scotland Yard inspector Guy Northeast. *They Rang Up the Police* (0-915230-27-5, $14.00) and *Death at The Dog* (0-915230-23-2, $14.00).

Glyn Carr. The 15 books featuring Shakespearean actor Abercrombie "Filthy" Lewker are set on peaks scattered around the globe, although the author returned again and again to his favorite climbs in Wales, where his first mystery, published in 1951, *Death on Milestone Buttress* (0-915230-29-1, $14.00), is set.

Torrey Chanslor. Sixty-five-year-old Amanda Beagle employs good old East Biddicut common sense to run the agency, while her younger sister Lutie prowls the streets and nightclubs of 1940 Manhattan looking for clues. The two inherited the Beagle Private Detective Agency from their older brother, but you'd never know the sisters had spent all of their lives knitting and tending to their garden in a small, sleepy upstate New York town. *Our First Murder* (0-915230-50-X, $14.95) and *Our Second Murder* (0-915230-64-X, $14.95) are charming hybrids of the private eye, traditional, and cozy mystery, published in 1940 and 1941 respectively.

Clyde B. Clason. *The Man from Tibet* (0-915230-17-8, $14.00) is one of his best (selected in 2001 in *The History of Mystery* as one of the 25 great amateur detective novels of all time) and highly recommended by the dean of locked room mystery scholars, Robert Adey, as "highly original." It's also one of the first novels to make use of Tibetan culture. *Murder Gone Minoan* (0-915230-60-7, $14.95) is set on a channel island off the California coast where a Greek department store magnate has recreated a Minoan palace.

Joan Coggin. Meet Lady Lupin Lorrimer Hastings, the young, lovely, scatter-brained and kindhearted daughter of an earl, now the newlywed wife of the vicar of St. Marks Parish in Glanville, Sussex. You might not understand her logic but she always gets her man. *Who Killed the Curate?* (0-915230-44-5, $14.00), *The Mystery at Orchard House* (0-915230-54-2, $14.95), *Penelope Passes or Why Did She Die?* (0-915230-61-5, $14.95), and *Dancing with Death* (0-915230-62-3, $14.95).

Manning Coles. The two English writers who collaborated as Coles are best known for those witty spy novels featuring Tommy Hambledon, but they also wrote four delightful—and funny—ghost novels. *The Far Traveller* (0-915230-35-6, $14.00), *Brief Candles* (0-915230-24-0, 156 pages, $14.00), *Happy Returns* (0-915230-31-3, $14.00) and *Come and Go* (0-915230-34-8, $14.00).

Lucy Cores. *Painted for the Kill* (0-915230-66-6, $14.95). A French refugee movie star's visit to an exclusive Manhattan beauty salon creates all kinds of havoc, especially when she wonders aloud before the newspaper photographers just how much breast it is okay to reveal in America. The salon's staff is falling all over themselves to insure that this publicity stunt doesn't backfire, while the salon's regular clients are feeling a bit ignored. But when this "French Lana Turner" is found dead under a very fancy mudpack, Captain Anthony Torrent, an English-born, ballet-loving homicide detective, is at a loss to understand why. After all, the victim just got out of Nazi-occupied France and, other than her traveling companion, doesn't really know a soul in America. Luckily, Torrent finds a helpful ally at the salon in the person of its very cynical exercise director, Toni Ney, who shares Torrent's love for both the ballet and solving murders. At first, Toni resists doing any sleuthing on her own but finally gives into temptation, aided by her boyfriend, Eric Skeets, a Spanish Civil War veteran now working as the salon's publicity director. First published in 1943, this is a sparkling comedy of manners laced with clues and jokes in equal measure. This edition restores all the original text from the original hardcover edition that was deleted from the wartime Dell Mapback reprint. *Corpse de Ballet* (0-915230-67-4, $14.95). Toni Ney's life has changed quite a bit since the events of *Painted for the Kill*. She's now writing an exercise column for a New York newspaper (the photo of her in a scanty exercise outfit is being carried around by a lot of GIs, much to the chagrin of her boyfriend, Eric Skeets, now a brand new second lieutenant waiting to go overseas) as well as serving as the paper's ballet reviewer. When a famous ballet dancer's long-awaited return to the stage ends in murder, Toni is on hand and once again in a position to offer an insider's point of view to Captain Torrent.

Norbert Davis. There have been a lot of dogs in mystery fiction, from Baynard Kendrick's guide dog to Virginia Lanier's bloodhounds, but there's never been one quite like Carstairs. Doan, a short, chubby Los Angeles private eye, won Carstairs in a crap game, but there never is any question as to who the boss is in this relationship. *The Mouse in the Mountain* (0-915230-41-0, $14.00), was first published in 1943 and followed by two other Doan and Carstairs novels, *Sally's in the Alley* (0-915230-46-1, $14.00), and *Oh, Murderer Mine* (0-915230-57-7, $14.00).

Elizabeth Dean. In Emma Marsh Dean created one of the first independent female sleuths in the genre. Written in the screwball style of the 1930s, *Murder is a Serious Business* (0-915230-28-3, $14.95), is set in a Boston antique store just as the Great Depression is drawing to a close. *Murder a Mile High* (0-915230-39-9, $14.00) moves to the Central City Opera House in the Colorado mountains.

Constance & Gwenyth Little. These two Australian-born sisters from New Jersey have developed almost a cult following among mystery readers. Each book, published between 1938 and 1953, was a stand-alone. The Rue Morgue Press intends to reprint all of their books. Currently available are: *The Black Thumb* (0-915230-48-8, $14.00), *The Black Coat* (0-915230-40-2, $14.00), *Black Corridors* (0-915230-33-X, $14.00), *The Black Gloves* (0-915230-20-8, $14.00), *Black-Headed Pins* (0-915230-25-9, $14.00), *The Black Honeymoon* (0-915230-21-6, $14.00), *The Black Paw* (0-915230-37-2, $14.00), *The Black Stocking* (0-915230-30-5, $14.00), *Great Black Kanba* (0-915230-22-4, $14.00), *The Grey Mist Murders* (0-915230-26-7, $14.00), *The Black Eye* (0-915230-45-3, $14.00), *The Black Shrouds* (0-915230-52-6, $14.00), *The Black Rustle* (0-915230-58-5, $14.00), *The Black Goatee* (0-915230-63-1, $14.00), and *The Black Piano* (0-915230-65-8).

John Mersereau. *Murder Loves Company* (0-915230-69-0, $14.95). James Yeats Biddle, a youngish professor of horticulture, is horrified when two very rare olive trees are killed during the 1939-1940 San Francisco Exposition on Treasure Island. Reporter Kay Ritchie and homicide inspector Angus McDuff are a bit more concerned with the murder of two Japanese laborers, whose bodies were hurled from a speeding automobile heading to the island on the Bay Bridge. Kay drags Professor Biddle, who is quite smitten with her, into a hunt for the murderer. It's a fascinating portrait of San Francisco on the eve of World War II as well as an early example of the use of horticulture in mystery fiction. First published in 1940. This title is scheduled for July 2004.

Marlys Millhiser. Our only non-vintage mystery, *The Mirror* (0-915230-15-1, $17.95) is our all-time bestselling book, now in a seventh printing. How could you not be intrigued by a novel in which "you find the main character marrying her own grandfather and giving birth to her own mother."

James Norman. The marvelously titled *Murder, Chop Chop* (0-915230-16-X,

$13.00) is a wonderful example of the eccentric detective novel. Meet Gimiendo Hernandez Quinto, a gigantic Mexican who once rode with Pancho Villa and who now trains *guerrilleros* for the Nationalist Chinese government when he isn't solving murders. At his side is a beautiful Eurasian known as Mountain of Virtue, a woman as dangerous to men as she is irresistible. First published in 1942.

Sheila Pim. *Ellery Queen's Mystery Magazine* said of these wonderful Irish village mysteries that Pim "depicts with style and humor everyday life." *Booklist* said they were in "the best tradition of Agatha Christie." Beekeeper Edward Gildea uses his knowledge of bees and plants to good use in *A Hive of Suspects* (0-915230-38-0, $14.00). *Creeping Venom* (0-915230-42-9, $14.00) blends politics, gardening and religion into a deadly mixture. *A Brush with Death* (0-915230-49-6, $14.00) grafts a clever art scam onto the stem of a gardening mystery.

Craig Rice. *Home Sweet Homicide* (0-915230-53-4, $14.95) is a marvelously funny and utterly charming tale (set in 1942 and first published in 1944) of three children who "help" their widowed mystery writer mother solve a real-life murder and nab a handsome cop boyfriend along the way. It made just about every list of the best mysteries for the first half of the 20th century, including the Haycraft-Queen Cornerstone list.

Charlotte Murray Russell. Spinster sleuth Jane Amanda Edwards tangles with a murderer and Nazi spies in *The Message of the Mute Dog* (0-915230-43-7, $14.00), a culinary cozy set just before Pearl Harbor. Jane runs roughshod over her family and the cops and, as usual, is forced to turn detective when brother Arthur is found at the scene of the crime, drunk (Jane insists—all evidence to the contrary—that Arthur has a delicate constitution and that one drink is all that is needed to render him senseless) and usually holding both incriminating evidence and a blonde. "Perhaps the mother of today's cozy."— *The Mystery Reader*.

Sarsfield, Maureen. These two mysteries featuring Inspector Lane Parry of Scotland Yard are among our most popular books. Both are set in Sussex. *Murder at Shots Hall* (0-915230-55-8, $14.95) features Flikka Ashley, a thirtyish sculptor with a past she would prefer remain hidden. It was originally published as *Green December Fills the Graveyard* in 1945. Parry is back in Sussex, trapped by a blizzard at a country hotel where a war hero has been pushed out of a window to his death, in *Murder at Beechlands* (0-915230-56-9, $14.95). First published in 1948 in England as *A Party for None* and in the U.S. as *A Party for Lawty*.

Juanita Sheridan. Sheridan's books feature a young Chinese American sleuth Lily Wu and her Watson, Janice Cameron, a first-time novelist. The first book

(*The Chinese Chop* (0-915230-32-1, 155 pages, $14.00) is set in Greenwich Village but the other three are set in Hawaii in the years immediately after World War II: *The Kahuna Killer* (0-915230-47-X, $14.00), *The Mamo Murders* (0-915230-51-8, $14.00), and *The Waikiki Widow* (0-915230-59-3, $14.00) .